D1556886

THE PENNY BOX

Price of Inheritance
The Silent Lady
Doctor Ross of Harton
The Story of Doctor Esmond Ross
Verdict of Doctor Ross
Dial Emergency for Doctor Ross
Don't Cage Me Wild
For I Have Lived Today
Message for Doctor Ross
Cry the Soft Rain
Reach for the Shadows
The Rainbow Glass
The Brass Islands
Prescription for Melissa
The Moonlit Way
The Strolling Players
The Diamond Cage
The Master of Jethart
The Gingerbread House
The Banshee Tide
The Glitter-Dust
Storm of Wrath
Lachlan's Woman
Danny Boy
The House of Jackdaws
The Chieftain

THE PENNY BOX

ALICE DWYER-JOYCE

ST MARTIN'S PRESS
NEW YORK

ROBERT HALE LIMITED
LONDON

© Alice Dwyer-Joyce 1980
First published in the United States
of America 1980

St Martin's Press, Inc.,
175 Fifth Avenue
New York, N.Y. 10010,
U.S.A.

Library of Congress Catalog
Card Number 80-51826

ISBN-0-312-60002-X

First published in Great Britain 1980

ISBN-0-7091-8535-9

Robert Hale Limited
Clerkenwell House
Clerkenwell Green
London, EC1R 0HT

Photoset by
Specialised Offset Services Limited, Liverpool
and printed in Great Britain by
Lowe & Brydone Limited
Thetford, Norfolk

To my patients, who became my
friends over many years as
a country G.P. in
Cambridgeshire

1

MARRAM

Looking back down the years, the first thing I can remember in life is the Penny Box. I still have it and count it of great value. It is a child's money-box, made of pottery, the head of a fisherman and a slit in the top of his sou'wester, where the pennies went in, if times were prosperous. I got him on the Christmas tree. I was about four years of age at the time, and straight away I gave him the honour of the centre of the living-room mantelpiece. He has always been a kind of good-luck piece. When I was young, I wove adventures about him. He seemed as alive to me as if he went out in the boat with Father, and he was very much part of the family. I imagine he still is.

He is a most reliable fellow with his seafarer's face, the grizzled beard along his jaw, the pipe between his teeth. My name is written on the blotting-paper texture of his base in a childish hand and protected with varnish against mortality. Mother always told me that she filled in XMAS and the date, for my skill did not go beyond my signature – Hillary Rudd.

I grew up and went out into the world, and time maybe battered both of us. I had, of course, mostly taken him with me. A long time afterwards somebody rescued him, perhaps tried to rescue me too. I had kept the missing pieces, and now they were replaced with great care, and he had a new paint coat and a fresh brush of varnish overall. It was hard to believe that it was not that Christmas Day so long ago, hard to believe that I was not as happy as a four-year-old child, but then possibly I was. I think the whole story revolves round the Penny Box Man. I am not likely to change my mind about him now.

My father, Noah Rudd, was a very important figure in the village where we lived, because he was Coxswain in the Marram Life-boat. When I sang 'Eternal Father, strong to save', aged about five, in church, on a night when a force eight gale was blowing north-easterly, and when the lifeboat had raced to sea down the slipway I was quite certain it was to him, we sang, had every confidence that our prayers would be answered, for had I not just heard the maroons and seen the launch of the *Adam, Seth and Joshua Rudd* hit the depth of the harbour at speed ... seen her bow split the ocean in two mighty waves, that stretched for the sky? My hand would feel clammy as I grasped Mother's, and we came to the last line and I knew the anxiety in her eyes, but we had reached the end of the hymn and must kneel down now.

Oh, hear us, when we cry to Thee
For those in peril on the sea ...

When I was a little older, I knew I had been praying to 'our Father, which art in Heaven'. It was one of the many confusions that time straightened out for me.

You might think that the Marram lifeboat had a strange

name, but it was a matter of pride to our family. Adam had been my grandfather, and Seth and Joshua had been my uncles, his sons. Adam had had three sons, the youngest, Noah, my father, only a teenaged lad, when the tragedy happened. Grandfather had been sixty-two years old and Coxswain. My uncles had· been grown men, but Father remembers how he wished he was 'growd up' and able to be one of the crew that night. I have heard about it often, how there was a sou'-easterly blow and an impossible sea. The lifeboat failed to appear at a rendezvous with some ship. There were no answering signals. She was found by an R.A.F. Shackleton at last, overturned ... The crew were lost, every one of them. So Margaret Rudd, my Gran, had lost her husband and two sons. She attracted the full sympathy of the nation, but she was a coxswain's wife. The village women looked at her only remaining son, a stripling lad ... looked at her dry eyes, asked her what she would do if Noah wanted to join 'the Service'. She had not hesitated. There was always a strong tradition in the Royal National Lifeboat Institution.

"If Noah should want to goo on the new lifeboat, when he's grow'd, I'll not stop him, nor try to."

And so it was.

I must get some order into my story, for it tosses me on the waves and floats me in and out with the tides.

Noah Rudd, my father, was any Norfolk fisherman, and I was any Norfolk lass. Marram was the smallest, neatest, most secret village you could find, because it was almost impossible to come to, and the coast-road traffic missed it. If you came south along the coast and that way, you are off the sea a bit. A long way after you left Hunston you had to turn to port, and the way to Marram was hard to find. If you did manage to find it, it turned into a dirt-track with many ruts in it, and this path turned and twisted about on itself and about again. Then there was a painted notice, *NO THROUGH ROAD*, and if that did not deter you, you came on an ill-written warning: *KEEP OUT. PRIVATE LAND. TRESPASSERS WILL BE PERSECUTED*, and I do mean 'persecuted'. Vandals had maltreated this notice. It was a tradition with the children to keep it looking as if visigoths lived hereabouts. Last of all, a very official Board of Works bill-board said *NO ENTRY TO THE SEA*, which was a downright lie, but I was always of the opinion that perhaps it was a place that had never been. It was certainly a paradise to me. Marram had stood still as the years passed by.

Perhaps a stranger found a way to get in, a time or two, but it was nigh impossible to find it twice running. They just did not make the effort. They left us in peace. If ever there was peace, it was here, in Marram-by-the-Sea.

Stand with me at the top of a rise and view a stage-setting. Below is a small perfect harbour with a few fishing-boats, a speed craft and the odd dinghy, bollards on the quay and lobster-pots and heaps of nets, or perhaps nets hung up to dry. Along the coast north was a white gate, and a path that led to a Martello Tower and its flag flying.

Then to the south of the harbour the start of a long stretch of sand-dunes rising to a craggy cliff, and along the sea a wood wall to hold the high tides back. Early on I thought these were Nelson's wooden wells of England.

Our cottage is on the top of the cliff, but it crouches down, underneath the crest of the coast, and anyhow, it

could not be called a cliff – not like at Mundesley. Behind
the dunes is the village proper, a small flint church with a
slate roof and stained-glass windows, 'Gothic' style
parochial school, dated 1880, where I started my formal
education. In the main street is the shopping-centre – the
Butcher's and the Grocer's. It's a Happy Family village. If
you held a pack of those cards in your hands, you could
encircle the whole parish ...

Mr. Grimes, the Butcher, and his wife and son and
daughter ... and so on ... Mr. Ship, the carpenter, and his
family ... Mr. Grimes again, but this time, Jimma Grimes,
Garage man, and his family, and the Butcher is his brother
... Mr. and Mrs. Pegg, the Grocers, and they sell the
morning newspapers in the afternoon ... Mr. Gooch and
son and daughter, for vegetables and fruit in season and
fresh eggs ... and Commander Robert Penn lives in the
Martello Tower, converted, but he is an object of mystery.

The lifeboat house and the slip commands the harbour,
but let me take you to our cottage first of all, which is at the
top of the rise of Sea Lane.

Otherwise there is nothing to the village but fishermen's
cottages, and they are in flint rows – and there is peace
here, but maybe I said that already. Our place of abode was
Flint Cottage which is converted from two cottages, an old
coast guard station. Two families used to live there, and
that is history, for it seems that the Rudds had always lived
there. There were two storeys to it, and a third floor with
two dormer windows, and it was my delight to be allowed
to take this top height of all the day I went to school. It
showed me that I had 'grow'd up' and perhaps it helped the
strain of a first day at school.

Father had a bunk built into the wall and had given me a brass binnacle lamp. If it was a stormy night and the lifeboat was out, I had that lamp burning in the window all night. There was an old brass telescope on a stand that turned – a map of the coast. I had a photograph of the *Adam, Seth and Joshua Rudd*. I had so many marine treasures – jetsam, flotsam, shells of infinite variety. No small girl, even if she lived in a castle, could have had such marine riches as I.

Best of all, the cottage faced due north, and I had only to look out of either of my two windows to see the North Pole star. I knew at the age of five that if I steered a boat straight to the North Pole Star from the sea below I might arrive at the North Pole itself, and that was a magic thing – or seemed so. If I managed to navigate the Pole, I could go straight on to Russia.

Sea Lane had a small rise to it, and the last house was ours. 'Flint by name and flint by nature' as Father said, but the cottage was cunningly laid out. It could still be identified as two houses and it had two twisting staircases. We lived in the starboard house, and Mother used the port side for her bakery shop. It had been started by Adam's wife, my grandmother, now retired to the chimney corner. My mother had taken it on, and Gran sometimes helped with the baking and sat in the shop to talk to the customers, if she began to think too much of the *Adam, Seth and Joshua Rudd*. She was no lone, lorn widow, such as Dickens wrote about in *Copperfield*. She had a face like a walnut, as to colour and wrinkles. Age had stooped her a bit. If you asked her how she was, her stock reply was 'not so bad'. She suffered from 'they screws', and that meant rheumatism in

Norfolk, but she 'warn't done fur a whiles yet'.

So on the left was this neat little shop and a display of fresh bread and the smell of baking, hot doughnuts too, with jam that might burn your mouth if you were too hungry to wait, puff-pastry apple turn-overs, and Mother's speciality, sticky, seedy, fruity buns. I can taste them yet.

The back room had the big oven and was a mouth-watering cave. The loaves were fetched out with a thing that might have been the oar of a coble. On a winter's day, with the north wind blowing a half gale and icy, it was the most comfortable place I knew. When I had left Marram and gone away and I came home for a holiday, and as I grew up, this back room seemed to shrink into itself and shrivel with time. It had been the finest place, but now I had seen many places that I thought finer. I realise that I was wrong. There was nothing on earth finer – nor will be.

Mother was a dumpling of a woman, perhaps a bit like Peggotty – a Norfolk Biffin, always with a spotless white apron, her sleeves rolled up to her elbows on floury arms, her hair in a pony tail with a tortoise shell clasp and a smile on her face. She and I had such a pride in Father. Always we watched the launch, unless it was well past my bed-time, and always my hand in hers. We were so sure that he would come safely home, even if the sea was like a corral of white horses and threatening to gallop over the face of the earth. I have strayed from the Penny Box again, so we must come back to Sea Lane, and this time we must seek out the living-room, which was in the starboard side of the cottage, as you faced the sea. Father had created a chimney-place for the living-room. The coast was plagued with erosion by the sea. Marram stood firm, but there were parts of Norfolk

13

that were yielding. Come a big storm and a few more yards
of the land would be surrendered. You had just to walk
along the sands at Lessingham to see whole houses
scattered down on to the beach. It put fear in your chest
that one day the sea would overwhelm Marram, but how
could it, because of all the long roots of the marram grass
that held faith – that and the small rise to the coast, where
Flint Cottage was. The Martello Tower too was on quite a
height and stood on rock, as a lighthouse might. Anyhow,
my father had taken it into his head to collect bricks from
cottages that lay washed by the sea on the coasts south of
us. The bricks were worn by salty tides and had turned a
paler pink and got a sea look to them. Father had built a
great chimney-piece that covered half the wall of the living-
room. He had used polished sea timber for the mantelshelf,
ten feet long and four inches deep of teak, and set the bricks
to make two hobs, where we could sit close by the fire.
There was an open hearth to take the jetsam we collected
from the shore. Wet from the sea, the wood would burn
brightly and send star-sparks up the chimney. Never must
we come up from the sands empty-handed. The wood was
stacked against the end wall of the house – our treasure
trove. There was always a pile of wood to hand for burning
in the winter, and more of it against the side wall of the
oven. The front of the living-room fire-place was bordered
by big matched flint cobbles, and it was wonderfully
wrought, but most important of all was the Penny Box that
was set right in the centre of the mantelshelf, signed by the
child's hand of Hillary Rudd. I had to stand on tiptoe to
reach it. If it rattled, it meant I had spending money. There
was a palette-knife to be fetched from the bakehouse to

extract the coin; and I have known the rich days when there was a threepenny piece, or even a little silver sixpence. Every day I shook the Penny Box Man, but usually there was no sound. I knew Father was more free with the money than Mother was, and she was the one that told me I must get more respect for saving for the future. Father laughed at her and told her not to be so hard on me. When I helped him with the accounts later on I was his 'book-keeper'.

"Can't you remember the starvation *you* had in your belly for bulls' eyes when you were five, Mary? It's not time for her to be starting her bottom drawer yet," he said to Mother.

Father would stand with the Penny Box in his hand, and I might know he had a coin in his pocket. He always turned the box over and read my child's signature and laughed.

"Hillary, and that's a shining flag sort o' name we give you. Sir William Hillary, 1771-1847 – the gentleman, who got the Royal National Lifeboat Service off the ground to what it became. Hillary of the Isle of Man. Of course, there had been lifeboats for a great many years, and many a rescue, but he breathed life into life-saving at sea. It's the voluntary part that counts. It's not government-run. It's given freely and it's bred into fisherfolk. It became an honour, so that when the maroons sound there will be men standing by, awaiting for the honour of crewing a lifeboat ... and great ladies raising the money for the expenses, and little children with a Lifeboat money-box in their hands ... maybe a dog at their feet ... and Lords willing to sign their names ... and families like your family, Little Fish, who are born into service ... and the honour of it."

He turned to me once and told me it was time I started

school. Gran and Mother were too busy to take me, but they had a fine new uniform ready for me. It was a green skirt and a white blouse and a green beret and the badge to it. If it was raining the next day, I'd have to have my sou'wester and my blue wellies. There was nothing to be feared of. I could whip any of the big boys with a hand tied behind my back, and had I not my new cabin in the attic to come back to? It was just a sort of first step out into the world. He imagined it would not be my last ... and the wry crooked smile he had. If you think of Spencer Tracy, you can picture my father – just the same quiet way to him for all his importance, broad-shouldered, greying a little, a laugh in his eyes and a look that denied any importance and made a mock of it. He took the Penny Box in his hand the next morning, and I was in the living-room with him when he pushed a whole shilling into the slit in the sou'wester.

"You borrow your ma's cook-house knife when you come home and fish out your fortune. Don't think I don't know how you break and enter like any burglar, but your mawther has it you're spend-thrift ... has it you ought to start a little ole Savings Bank ... has it that money burns a hole in your pocket. That 'ud be the day. There ain't a woman in this house with the courage to go to school with you today without crying woman's tears over you, but reckon I know Hillary Rudd ..."

"It's a silly name for a girl," I interrupted. "I'd rather have been Dawn or Gloria."

"You're likely live to be older than your Gran," he laughed, and the pipe between his teeth. "A fine Dawn or Gloria you'll be then, if you don't remember to put your teeth in, a time or two, like your Gran don't ... can't see how she forgets 'em ... found them on the top of the mangle, just now ... daresay she was giving her gums a rest, bless her.''

School was an old-fashioned building at the bottom of Sea Lane – a parochial school, which had withstood modern education. I thought it was owned by the Vicar, who went there every day and sang hymns and said 'Our Father'. It had two class-rooms divided by a sliding glass partition, into juniors and seniors. The glass windows were set so high that you could not see out, only for the chestnut trees, which clothed the sky. There were no diversionary activities, only the murmur from the senior class next door. We had two teachers to about two score of children. I found it an agreeable institution. It had advantages. You could keep Polly-Wiggles, which were tadpoles, there in the spring and let them loose as frogs in the dew-pond in Farmer Pearson's paddock. Before Christmas, there were strips of coloured paper, and you pasted them together to make decorations for the festive season, took them home, too, on the last day of term, and Gran mumbled that they were nought but 'rubbitchy nonsense'.

"Welcome to Marram School, Hillary Rudd," Miss Meadows said that day. She was the young teacher and took the junior class, so I was in her care, aged five, with a head of copper hair, straight and cut to a fringe.

"Your Dad tells me you're their little book-keeper. You'll have to watch out for the sums."

She looked at him out of the corner of her eyes, her cheeks pinkish.

"I saw you arrive down the lane with Hillary on the

17

cross-bar of your bike, Coxswain. I reckon you thought you were launching the lifeboat with the speed you were going and we really don't approve of it on that corner. P.C. Gawthrop will be after you, if you don't watch out. The next thing you'll get up to will be piracy and smuggling. I always think you're cut out for a smuggler."

She smiled at him, for she liked him. Everybody liked Father.

"Don't look so worried," she grinned. "I'll not report you and I'll take care of your 'little fish' for you. My word! Doesn't she stand brave to the world? She's a chip off the old block, just like her father and her gramp before her and not afraid of man nor yet beast."

How wrong she was! I had terror in the pit of my stomach, for I knew that there was something 'they' did to 'new sproggs'. I sat in the front row in front of Billy Grimes, the Butcher's son, and at break he baptised me with a bottle of very old milk that smelt sour. 'Copper Head', he named me, and that stuck right through to my College days. I thought it a fine name till I learned that a copper-head was a snake.

"Bless you," everybody said. "Your hair looks polished like silk – smashing! It's as bright as ship's brass."

Maybe they were wrong. Maybe I was a snake. There was a time when I fell into a snake-pit.

Just for now I was in the front row of the class, and Billy Grimes had some wood-lice in a small sweet bag and he was trying to put them down the back of my blouse. After my baptism he was at the same teasing ploy, and I whispered to him to lay off. I gave him warning, but he took no notice. It was a moment's work to turn round, but it was

18

a pity his nose bled so much. We spent the afternoon, he in one corner of the class-room and I in another, and my hair still smelt of sour milk. I washed it out in the sea before I went home ... said school was super and got the knife out of the shop to extract my silver shilling, from the Penny Box, bought a twist of sweets for each of my folks. I was so happy to be home again. I remember getting wine-drops for Gran to strengthen her gums, because her teeth were so bothersome. Those were the days!

So passed the formative years of innocence. It was a perfect background for a child such as I. I was as much part of the sea as any barnacle on the rocks.

In winter, the village snailed into its shell. Visitors went inland. The old retired pensioners from other parts stayed by their fires. We sat out the storms, with a fine feeling of safety. We were indeed a small community now. The gales were sudden and cruel on that coast, tossing the spume right over Flint Cottage. Even the sand-dunes could not hold formation against them. Sand shifted the face of the shore into a new pattern.

Ships made a passage along the coast about three miles out, and Father called it a Sea-Lane, just like ours. I watched the sea through my brass telescope and waited on the rough days for the boom of the maroons. It happened more often in the winter, and I knew the drill. In summer, it might be a child's rubber boat floated out to sea, or a swimmer in difficulties with the ebbing tide, but in the stormy days and nights of winter the demons rode the winds. I was accustomed to the drill. Father would get out his bike and race away down the lane. Mother and I held the gap in the cliff, and we had an old pair of binoculars.

The dull boom-boom of the maroons and three minutes flat and the Coxswain would have reached the Lifeboat House.

"Eternal Father, strong to save ..."

The crew would assemble, and fifteen men might be waiting for seven crew wanted. There was the *Adam, Seth and Joshua Rudd*, all ready to go, with the rows of gear in order, the slip-way ready and the pin waiting for the hammer-blow. It was amazing the speed she achieved on the slip. It was a praise to God the way the sea parted in front of her bows. Then she was across the harbour bar and away, and there would be lights out to sea. I knew the chattering of the intercom and thought of the days of Grace Darling when there had been nothing but courage.

I always held Mother's hand in mine and was well aware that she prayed too, for we both knew the sea by this – knew there were freak waves and impossible seas.

'Eternal Father, strong to save ...' but He had not saved Adam and Seth and Joshua ... had not stopped my father from going into the Lifeboat service, but I knew there was no choice open to him. If I had been a boy I'd have set out to be in any crew that went down the slipway. I had just 'to be grow'd enough', and maybe they would let ladies go to sea by then.

It might be hours long, the vigil, and then the winches would be drawing the boat up. Father was responsible for the good order and the cleanliness, for the readiness. The ship must be hosed down with fresh water and every item of gear too. There was always the chance of that double boom-boom again, as if a plane had split the sound barrier.

Looking back, it was never anything but sunshine and

summer, yet I clearly remember walking home from school with four others, all of us legs, under a great golfing umbrella, hoping the rain-squall would not lift us all over the rise. We walked the puddles with drilled deliberation, trusting in our wellies, and had a great game of splashing water into each other's boots.

It was a perfect happiness for a child, that piece of the coast. We had a foreshore of three miles of strand to our few selves. We had rock pools and cobbled flints. We had shells and coloured jewelled stones. There was even a mussel-bed at low tide, and it was fun to gather them for tea. It was fun to go shrimping, pushing a net like a miniature snow plough.

Father had a basement cellar at the back of the house that Mother did not approve of. It did not go with baking, she said. The bait for fishing was prepared there, and Father kept all his clobber there, gutted fish and so forth, and got the crab – and the lobster-pots ready. We had a stout sea-going craft at anchor in the harbour, and I was as good as two hands in the boat, or so Father said, but I think that he meant four. I was his partner, and he took me fishing in the holidays ... caught strange-looking creatures sometimes ... star-fish, things like small perfect flowers. Crabs and lobsters were best. They sold well, but I never could abide the way they had to be stored in wood boxes in the sea and their nippers tied.

There was a hard side to fishing, with the gutting of the fish in that basement and the bait to be prepared and everything kept spotless.

I was sick to my stomach at the bait at first, but I grew accustomed to it, and I was never sea-sick.

"It's nothing to get big-headed about," Father said. "It's an accident of birth. Some of the best sailors were seasick – ones like Nelson. Even in our own day they say Her Majesty don't fancy a rough sea in *Britannia.*"

I reckon I knew every inch of the coast for three miles in both directions before I was seven. I could swim like a fish, and I was burnt dark brown by the weather. I had a dog called Skippy, who was my constant companion, a small smooth Jack Russell, brown and white, who would never let me out of his sight. He took me to school every day after that first day. Every afternoon he waited at the school gate for me to come out. He and I explored every last bit of the parish up to a mile inland. Always we stuck in sight of the sea, but there was one part that was secret from us. If we walked north along the path from the harbour it led to a white gate and a notice to say that trespassers would be prosecuted, and there was no right of way and all the usual stuff. This was the gate to the Martello Tower that stood on a rise of rock to a cliff edge. There was a gentleman who lived there, and he was a loner. I knew that his name was Robert Penn, for he had to come down to the village for his newspapers and his shopping, but he never spoke to me, just smiled and touched the shiny peak of his cap. I saw his name on the top of *The Times* paper, and anyhow the people knew him as Robert Penn, Esquire. Even the most gossipy woman could tell me nothing about him, only that he had inherited the Martello Tower from his family and 'had done it up hisself'. There was a vague kind of whisper that he's have no woman aboard, and the men of Marram were unanimously of the opinion that he showed good sense in that.

He spoke in an English accent like the Television. The fishermen said he was a proper gentleman 'even in his dirt', and that meant his working-clothes, rust or blue slacks in sail-cloth, white high-necked sweater, seaman's cap. He was not often on view, only when he took his speed-boat across the sea or spent some time tinkering with her engine in the harbour. He did not encourage conversation. Father knew him well and told me that he had done the old Tower up a treat. There were three decks to it and a spiral stair running plum straight up the centre. I knew that there was a platform on the very top that had a ship's rail and an old cannon and a telescope. There was a flag that was flown every day and lowered at sunset. He had been something in the Navy in real life. Father said that maybe he had been shipwrecked, and if he had it was his own business not mine. If there was one thing 'The Commander' could not abide it was dogs. He had a red setter, and he didn't want her 'worrited', Father told me. Skippy and I were to stand off.

One day, I climbed the white gate and knew myself a trespasser, but I had an insatiable curiosity, and I had the excuse of being caught in a sudden squall, from the north-east, that drenched both Skip and me in five minutes flat. Anyhow, I had an excuse not to do as I was told. Robert Penn opened the door when he saw me coming along the path and asked me if I had seen a red setter bitch. I shook my head and told him not to worry, if it was Rouge he thought he'd lost.

"There's no traffic hereabouts," I reminded him. "She's a sporting dog and she won't mind the weather. She's a very friendly bitch. She always stops and passes the time

23

of day with me and Skippy."

"It's not you I'm afraid of," he said. "And how old are you?"

I said I was ten, and he asked me if I had not learned to read yet.

"I presume you saw the notice on my gate? Good God! Are you not able to read, and are you not aware that it's owing to the fact that my bitch *is* friendly that I'm worrying about her?"

"But there's nobody that would steal a fine animal like she is," I said. "Norfolk folk is honest."

"I'm not afraid of losing her. Don't you know ...? No, I daresay you don't, but now I see you're Noah Rudd's girl and adrift in a squall. You have far more right that I'll ever have had to this stretch of coast. Come in to my fire and get dry. Usually I don't encourage visitors, and this doesn't give you grace and favour to call when the mood takes you. Just this once then ..."

I had been told never to talk to strange men, especially if they promised me sweeties, but then he was not a stranger, and I forgot all the advice ever given me. The hail was stinging my face and I was cold. Skippy whined a little and kept close to my legs.

I cast an eye aloft to the flag and remarked that I was glad to see that he had the Union Jack right ways up.

"Right ways up!" he said, with a laugh. "Do you know what your Father told me about you. He says you're like the lifeboat. He says you're self-righting. He says that life will never overturn you ... that you'll always be self-righting. That's a fine faith he has in his 'little fish', and I see he's a good judge of character."

He had thrown open the door of the tower and stood aside to let me squelch into the fine hall. I walked in, Skippy still glued to my heels, and stopped short and stood and gaped at the staircase that spiralled right to the top of the tower. It was polished wood, and it was all runners and no risers, so that the whole was open to vision, winding round and round. There were three decks. You could call them nothing else, so nautical they were, circular beautiful rooms – edged and bounded with white rope rails.

Six steps up, and another six, and I was on the first floor. There was a big open fire burning in the grate, and the walls were mostly books. There was a captain's table in mahogany with a concave surface to conquer the tilting of the sea. The armchairs were leather and as deep as the ocean – dark green. The galley was to one side, and everything clipped into security. There were lockers and ships' lamps, and on the floor above bunks in the walls and cabins that were private, and you could see by the inside doors that they were high-ranking cabins.

I was mesmerised by the cups and glasses and bottles in one section of the ground floor, in a long dresser. I felt that we could get out to sea even in the present weather and not a thing would shatter or break. It was the first time I had seen a ship's decanter that could never overturn.

There was a great heap of drift-wood beside the fire and a pile of block peat out of the Broads. I could smell the fragrance of it as he threw on six bricks of it and no regard to the cost.

"I'll get you a cup of Bovril and a doorstep of bread with butter and cheese ..."

He was amused at himself for having taken in my small

self, yet he had seen the wonder in my eyes.

"Kick your boots off. They're full of sea. Your coat is soaked too, and the dog's nigh drowned. What breed is he? For heavens' sake, get close to the fire and warm."

I was enveloped in a cloud of steam as I squatted in front of the glow.

"Skippy's Jack Russell," I said. "He's a great guard-dog. If you was to attack me, he's as like as not bite you."

"I'll bribe him with some of the bitch's butcher's flat bones. She's taken up with a dog, south down the coast. I'll have to go out and look for her presently. It's usually that labrador in the news-shop, the chap that goes swimming every day in the harbour by himself."

We were very content by the fire and the steam rising round us, Skippy and I.

The storm blew itself out, and I did not presume on his hospitality. I said I must go home, and thanked him for having us, went away down his drive and turned to wave farewell to him. I thought he looked very forlorn standing there by himself.

He watched me all the way down the path, and I had promised to look out for his missing setter. I had also suggested that I contacted the labrador dog at the newspaper shop, but he said it was not a woman's work. He tried hard to keep a straight face, when he said it. I had even offered to come and visit him a time or two, but he advised me not to.

"That notice means what it says," he assured me. "I don't want to have to prosecute Skippy."

That evening I lay in my bunk and worried as usual that my breasts seemed to be budding. I had asked Mother about this and if I was getting too fat, but she told me it was the way of nature. I was growing up and must expect such things and not to worry. Worry killed the cat! I was early, but then when had I been late for anything since the day I was born? It was good that I had come to her, if there was something on my mind.

"I think maybe you have a year or two yet, Copper, but one day you'll leave off being a child. You'll be a woman, like Gran or myself – with all the burdens life puts on us women."

She sighed.

"Reckon it's just that we lost happiness in the Garden of Eden, but be proud when you feel grow'd up. Father is such an old fool that he'd put you to crewing the lifeboat, but don't put any trouble in his lap, count of being a grow'd woman. There is a new set of rules women have these days. I don't know what girls is coming to."

I did not know what she was talking about, and when I went to bed I put my thoughts firmly back on Robert Penn. I entered a magic land and fell in love with him. It was soon done. I had just to think of the Martello Tower and the spiral of shining steps and that silver fair hair of his and his eyes like clear blue glass, and the gentle way he had. Maybe I had never met anybody like him before, but he had been kind to me, and he had respected my childishness. He had not insulted my ignorance by explaining rudely that his bitch was on heat, but I should have known about such matters. He steered clear of the harsh things of life. That night I created a new world for myself, where he and I walked together, in the fantasia, that comes between sleep and waking. We lived on a desert island alone together, and one adventure built on another and ran from night to night. I might have taken a coble and rescued him from shipwreck. I might be his wife in the Martello Tower. I might darn his socks and obey his every whim. I might please him or maybe displease him. I thought that, gladly, I might have died for him. It went on for many years, but he was unaware of it, only that perhaps I haunted him a bit. I prayed that he would invite me to the Tower, but he never did. I crept in there and left a gift lobster quite often. I lied myself out of it when Father asked me why Penn was always thanking him for anonymous lobsters.

I was eleven. I was twelve. I was thirteen. I moved up into the senior half of the school beyond the glass partition. I was Miss Woodhouse's pupil now, and she was very different from Miss Meadows. She was elderly to my eyes at least, and grey-haired. She was vinegary. She was an idealist. She had no husband or children, and the school was her life. She was always delving in the earth for a diamond. One day she might drill into a child's composition and come on oil in the bore. 'The corn is green' – was that it? Was it Emlyn Williams who wrote that powerful novel about the Welsh mining valleys? Had he been the actor and had Cronin written the book? I had not even heard of it, but I remember it now. It moved the heart to breaking ...

Miss Woodhouse saw the flow of oil from the drill. Maybe she thought she had hit it rich in me. She was determined 'to get me on'. She gave me extra lessons after school. She lent me books – Dickens and Trollope and then Shakespeare. She opened poetry to me, and not 'I wandered lonely as a cloud' and the metre beaten out on

28

the desk with a ruler. I went for poetry, and she thought she had won. She could never know that I was weaving John Donne into Robert Penn and my eyes heavy with sleep. I drowned in poetry – Elizabeth Browning and her great story and 'How do I love thee … let me count the ways … I shall but love thee better after death …', and then in my real life I escaped drowning by a miracle. Gran said I was 'allus a body that did something ork'ard', and indeed I did it that time.

It was the day after the big storm, and the loss of a trawler in Haisborough Sands.

Well I knew of Happisborough village, and ten miles out there were 'Haisborough sands', with the reputation of being far more full of wrecks than the Goodwins. It puzzled me that the sands and the village had a similar sound to their names, but only the native élite knew it. The shallows have more ships in their grave than any sands I know.

The maroons had gone at midnight, and Father was away. I got up to meet his return to Flint Cottage at the first light.

"We got them all off safe, Little Fish, but she's a write-off – a Spanish trawler – and they might have talked Double Dutch for all we could understand what they were trying to say, and that went both ways. We had to pluck them out of her rigging. We sailed right alongside, but there was no making them jump down to our deck. I prised the captain off the bridge myself, and it was like getting a cockle off a rock. He might have drowned us all, but he would not desert his ship. It's a bad thing to watch your ship die."

I made his breakfast and got him to bed, asked him if he had seen Skippy down by the harbour, but he said not. He fell into bed and was asleep, and I went out to see the day. The storm was easing now and the sky red from dawning. The sea was angry still. I whistled to Skippy, but that did not make him come. I turned south towards Happisborough, though it was miles and miles out of distance for vision of anything else. Here was a stretch of the coast to the south that consisted of high sand-dunes. The Council had built a sea wall – a sea defence that was contrived with groynes that reached from the sea-wall down to beyond low tide-line. It sectioned the shore into oblongs of perfect sands about two hundred yards wide. The trouble was that the tides could shift the sands along to north or south. Now and again there was a concrete step that you could climb from sand to sea-wall, but there were sections where no steps existed. There were spaces that could come to be traps as the tides came in if the current had scooped sand out.

There was a fine walk along the sea-wall along the firm strong concrete. If a child or a dog were to go down to one of these sections and the tide were to run in fast there could be deep water and no way up to the sea-wall. The sea had been vicious enough for the last twenty-four hours to shift the sands anywhere ... and Skippy was always at home in the mornings ... and still I could whistle into the wind and no sign of him. I do not know why I ran south. I might see drift-wood, but that was usual after such a night. We would have wood for the collecting for our winter fires. The tide was not full. The water-level was well down from the sea-wall. I set off with the wind at my back, and worried a little for the sections with no steps to the sea-wall were filling to danger. Where was Skip? The waves were great rollers that were breaking against the concrete. There was a four-foot drop from below where my feet hurried to the waves that sent the spume over my head. Close to the wall it was churning the usual floating rubbish. The sky was grey pink and the clouds racing. Out to sea were the white horses, and the wind was in my back, as if it urged me that there was no time left.

There had been dogs that had drowned on this sort of day. I put my fingers in my mouth and whistled again, but the wind blew the sound to nothing. I tugged my anorak hood down round my face and tied the string tightly and set off again at a trot.

Then after a long time I saw him coming to meet me, and all my worry fell away. He ran at full gallop and greeted me with barking and nipped at my ankles, and I knelt down to gather him into my arms. His tongue licked at my face. Then he broke away from me ... was off down the coast at full speed, stopped up short and yelped at me, and when I tried to get him he was off again, and he was so wet with the sea that he might have been swimming – and now I knew the deep sections with no steps. God knows Skippy tried to tell me, but I was angry with him because he refused to turn home with me. He was away at the next groyne, and when I reached that he was away again and back to dance round me and nip my ankles again. Just where we stood there was a groyne and no steps to either side of it, but now the water was lapping almost to my feet, and he was off on another dash ahead of me, and I could not turn him. There was nothing to do but go pelting after him, and I was glad the wind was in my back for it had started to hail. There was another groyne coming to meet the sea-wall and it made a

31

turbulent angle to the concrete. The sea-level was four feet down, and it swirled with planks from ships' timbers and all the usual stuff – plastic containers, odd shoes, empty tins, floating glass bottles, loose strands of sea-weed and onions from some lost cargo, a lone electric light bulb. I stood looking down at the angle for a little time before I saw the creature that was thrown below my feet. It was a dog, and it was maybe dead – no, its eyes looked at me, and its paws paddled very feebly, then it was gone under again, but in that one short glimpse I recognised the drowned ruddy hair. It was the red setter from the Tower. I knelt down on the concrete, and Skippy stood at my side with too much faith in my power. I lay flat and reached down, but could come in no way near enough to the level of the water at its height. I stretched my hand down and screamed at Rouge to try to swim to me, but she was past hearing. There was a current from the north that battered her against the sunk line of the groyne. If I could get it through to her to swim against the current, yet I knew the water was not high enough to grasp her by the scruff of the neck, I'd have to get her to go to the groyne I had just passed. Skippy looked up at me and maybe he said goodbye to me. He jumped high and wide into the white swirl of the water, and in a long moment his head appeared, and her head too, and they were tossed like dice in a gambler's hand among all the flotsam.

I stood up and looked up and down the coast, but there was no sign that Marram was inhabited. There was no sign of a cottage or a lone walker. I could barely see the harbour, could not make out any detail. With luck, the Air Sea Rescue Helicopter might be due, but the lowering clouds were empty. I knelt down, lay flat down and stretched out my hand, tried to make the dogs swim back to the next groyne north – but perhaps Rouge was dead. No, there she was again, and Skippy with her, and she was completely helpless now, and God help Skippy! He stayed closed to her. I took off my anorak and threw it up the grass, kicked off my boots and discarded my wool dress. I shivered in pants and bra – the bra that I was so proud of, for it meant I was a woman at last, like Mother and Gran. I was just fourteen turned.

I saw Rouge sink, and dived for her and caught her in the dive. There was a cable that floated in all the rubbish, and I grabbed it. I must get out to the smoother water, from this turmoil, but first I had to fashion a lead for Rouge or she was lost. I tried to concentrate on seaman's knots. I got a good enough lead about her neck. I struck out to sea and back north along the coast, called to Skippy to come too, and we were a strange convoy. Time slowed down. At least we were out of immediate danger, or were we? A floating plank took me in the temple and the blood was warm down my face, but out here the sea was calmer. Rouge was like the ship's captain last night, I thought. She would not abandon ship. I had to prise her off the groyne, and now I was a tug and she had been taken in tow. Skippy was the escort vessel. I laughed to myself, with no laughter in me, and a sea took me full in the face and knocked my imagination out of me for a while. The cable drew Rouge close to me, and Skippy stood by, but their claws tore my shoulders. The sea was pinkish with my blood, and Skippy licked my neck as an apology.

I tried to review the situation. On the next groyne the

sea-level was such that I could lean up and reach the wall. It was a two hundred yards swim, say a bit more, for we had to come in shore. The current was in our teeth with the full strength of the North Sea. I made headway, but not much. I prayed for Sam to come, and he'd have Joe with him in the Air Sea Rescue Helicopter, yet the whirly bird propellers might sink the whole convoy of us. I trusted Sam and Joe. Joe would come down on the winch. "Eternal Father, strong to save ..." I said, and I was tired now. It would be so very easy to stop, to let go the cable and roll over and down to sleep. Then the hail started again and slapped my face, and Skippy had had enough. He whined to me to do something. I reached to stroke his wet head.

"We'll come ashore at the next groyne. I can reach the sea-wall there, Skippy ... we'll get home for breakfast ... then maybe a walk ..."

God help him! I saw the wag of the stump of his tail, and he licked at my face and tore my shoulders again, woke me up. We had won, thank God, we had won. We were within measuring reach of the sea-wall and the water lapping the top of it.

Then I looked for the last time out to sea as I struck in again for the shore. There was a wall of breaking wave coming in about two hundred yards out, ten feet high and destroying and tumbling all about it – a great holocaust of a breaker, a freak, a bank of tossing white foam, but I recognised death when I saw it. We could not survive it even with victory in our grasp. I caught Skippy by the scruff of his neck. I tightened my hand near her collar against Rouge's head. I trod water and I shut my eyes. Coward that I was, I shut my eyes and prayed that Jesus accept our three souls. Dogs must have souls too. I was done in, it was a big effort to move my arms any more. I felt myself lifted into the power of the breaker. I felt myself cast forwards – felt concrete skin my knees bare. Then there was wet grass under me and I was on a small rise of sand-grass, and the dogs tight in my hands still. I pulled them up the slope, and they were not dead and neither was I. We were lying safe from the cruel sea but the hail still flailing down on us, and it was cold ... cold ... cold ...

There was nothing to do now but walk home with the dogs, and I knew I would be in trouble. I had broken every rule of the sea. I would have to answer for it at Flint Cottage.

It was so very cold. It might have been mid-winter, but Skippy was sitting up and licking his coat. Then he stood up, tried to shake himself and staggered a little. He went over to smell Rouge's black nose, and I turned my attention to her ... closed my hands tight round her muzzle and breathed deep into her. It was like magic the way she took my breath and made a life of it, out of death. But I was so very cold, and there was more than a mile between me and the cottage. I stood up, staggered, and sat down again. I must get the dogs home. Maybe they would go home by themselves, but they crept close to me, and trembled – in every limb.

I fixed Skippy with my eyes and told him to fetch Father, but he would not go. I began to start the slow climb on my hands and knees along the marram grass, a dog at each side of me. In twenty yards I was deadly sick, and I felt better. I got to my feet and staggered along the sea-wall, hating the sea that still reached for my bare feet. I had lost my socks

35

somewhere, and there would be trouble about that too. They were new – were supposed to last out the winter. There was all the expense of new clothes for the next term, and we were not rich. I thought of the Penny Box. If I saved up the money from it, and did without sweets, I might be able to buy the new socks and not let Gran know.

Oh God! It was so cold, and the blood was streaking my face and running down my chest.

There was a man on the sea-wall, and he ran when he saw us. I saw the silver hair and knew Robert Penn, who could only be out looking for Rouge.

It was all very confused.

"She's safe, Mr. Penn. She got down on the shore, where there are no steps and the sand had been swept out last tide. Skippy went in after her, so I went in too. They're all right – so am I."

Then I remembered my nakedness and wanted to hide myself ... felt a great shame. His coat was round me, and he was putting my arms in the sleeves. He was gone five minutes and then back again and rum in my mouth and his arms round me. The dogs were able to wag their tails too, but they were as apologetic as I.

I felt his arms round me, supporting me. I tried to tell him what had happened. Rouge had got caught in a section without steps ... we had been a kind of convoy ... Skippy had jumped in and I had had no choice but to go in after them both. Skippy was the brave one. I'd likely get into trouble for going against all the rules.

I remember half-way home he stopped up short and took my shoulders between his hands.

"There'll be no trouble. You walked your family's steps today. It's only that your ship changed course for a fair voyage. I can promise you happiness for the rest of your life for what you just did. God damn me if I don't see you get it! You're a woman in a hundred thousand and the breeding to match what you've just done ..."

And then, more softly,

"Now it's time for bed and great honour to you and no blame. Didn't your forebears offer their lives willingly to save lives, but you, you, you ... you chose to pick the life of two dogs, and one of them mine. I knew the first day I saw you that you were chartered for fame. You threw your life away just to save two dogs."

I was sitting up in the living-room before the fire, wrapped in a thick red blanket, drinking hot milk. Gran was muttering to herself that it were 'a lot of rubbitch', but nobody listened to her. It was then that my life changed. I did not recognise it as the time, but I know it now.

Perhaps I imagined that Robert Penn leaned down and spoke to me again.

"Now your name will go up in lights. They'll not let you escape publicity – not with your history and you, a child yet. Fourteen years of age ..."

He sighed and went on to say that the world was starved for such stuff as I was made of.

"I'm not a child. Fourteen is grow'd enough. I'm for a new school soon."

"You'll have to run the gauntlet of publicity first, or I think so. For a start accept the freedom to come and go as you please to the Martello Tower. You're welcome to ignore the 'no trespassers' sign. It's the least I can do for the service you've done me today. No harm will ever come to you in my house."

"Don't put dreams in her head," Father said laughing.

"Her life will be very occupied. She's for a day school in Norwich in two weeks and no nonsense about it. Miss Woodhouse has great hopes of her, and she nearly put paid to them today."

Father came to speak to me in confidence when I was in bed and asked me to tell him all that had happened. I told him as best I could recall it and Skippy fast asleep against my side under the eiderdown.

"I broke the rules," I said. "But down on the shore there was nothing else I could do. I know there's a lifebelt on a pole thereabouts, but it was a long way. There was no time for Rouge if I went for it. I threw my red anorak high on the grass and hoped somebody would see it, see the rest of my things too and look for me. It was all I could think to do. Was I wrong when I went in after them? There was no hope left, and it was Skip too. Skip would have jumped in after me if I'd gone in first."

He held me in his arms as if he had lost me and found me again, and his voice was husky.

"Little Fish! Little Fish! I'd have done exactly as you did. If I were you and it happened just so, and if I managed to find the courage, but don't you do it again – ever. It was a long haul. The sea could have smashed you against the groyne, and it was running just right to do it. You knew that too. Didn't you?"

I nodded my head, and said if I did not I soon realised it, but there was no joking left in him.

"Don't ever do it again," he said. "You have to weigh the cost of every action at sea. There's a kind of invisible scales, and the weights the prevailing conditions. Either you saved the lives of two dogs or maybe only one, but you know that part of the dunes and it were a big gamble. If you hadn't made it, there'd have been total loss of the crew. You never gave it a thought, did you? Just think of it now, Flint Cottage, and what the big fireplace downstairs would be like with no Copper. Just picture the Penny Box Man and no hand to reach for him. You threw yourself into the scales, and you threw your mawther and your Gran and me. Gran may seem a bit hard on you at times, but she sets a great store by you. Don't tell me she annoys you with the way she leaves her teeth on the mangle, but she only does that to 'aereate' you. You should take no notice of it and she'd soon stop. There's times I think you don't appreciate Gran and the stuff she's made of. If you ask me, I think of all the family you take after her – chip of the old block. There's a picture of her at your age, and you're the dead spit of her – picture a bit faded now. Reckon she'd ha' died if you'd been brung in drowned ..."

He tucked in the blankets and went to the door.

"God forgive me! I'd have taken the Penny Box Man and smashed him against the back of the chimney, with the thought of never seeing your hand reach for him and the hope alive in your face, never to see it no more. There would have been no happiness left for any one of us, not till the end of time."

It was strange the way it came about. Just for now I was surprised at the tears on his face.

2

HALE'S OF NARBOROUGH

I was out of bed and dressed by dinner-time, but I had no appetite for the stewed steak and 'swimmers' Gran made, though usually I polished my plate. I fed Skippy with most of it under the table, and then helped with the washing-up. It was after that, that the reporter came from the *Eastern Daily Press*, and he brought a photographer with him. He wanted to see me and he wanted to see Skippy, and he came in when invited, and both of the men were very friendly. They had tea and sticky buns, and we talked about the 'sea rescue', as they called it. He was very concerned about the fact that a strong tide could and did sweep the sand from one section of the defences to another and leave what he called 'a drowning pit'. The Council had been negligent not to put escape steps in each stretch. He would promise me personally that such conditions would never arise again when the *Eastern Daily Press* 'told the world' about it.

As for me, did I realise what a brave girl I was? He took me down to the shore, and we talked a great deal. Then the photographer took pictures of the sands and of me and of Skippy. Then we went back to Flint Cottage and took more pictures. He left us after tea and went on to the Martello

Tower to fit Rouge into the story, and he shook my hand before they went.

"My God!" he said. "I'm glad I went down to the place and saw it for myself. I didn't realise till I saw how it looked, like run-away white horses. I'd not have jumped in there for a hundred dogs."

He was a Scot and a very pleasant man. He looked through the car window at me.

"You've given me the nuts and the bolts to build a fine story. We'll have six sets of steps along that stretch and no necessity for a fourteen-year-old girl to throw her life away. There's been enough of giving in your family."

In my next term at school I was to see magnesium flare in chemistry class. It reminded me of the days that were almost upon me now. I went up in a brilliant flash of glory and I really did not understand how it came about. They were comparing me to Grace Darling, and I smiled at the interviewer who came all the way from Anglia T.V. studios in Norwich. I was astonished when I saw myself on the screen.

"I'm nothing like Grace Darling. She was brave," I said. Gran had told me to 'act natural', and maybe I did. I need not have worried about Gran's teeth. She was my main cause of concern, and she looked lovely in her black dress and the lace collar.

"She did nothing that weren't expected of her," she said. "Mebbe the day will come when I'm proud of her yet."

We went over big, or so they told us, and more and more people were involved. I hit the world press, for it was a slack season for news. Then the R.N.L.I. were after me like a hawk after a dove, but so much mercy in them. The

42

Woman's Navy tried to tempt me to think of a career in the W.R.N.S. eventually. I wondered what I had wandered into. I soon knew. My whole life had been swung to a star.

By a freak of luck, there was a famous boy's public school throwing open its door to girls. Thirty girls had been picked to be allowed into hallowed cloisters. One of the girls at the last moment had been withdrawn. Her parents had been posted to Switzerland for a Common Market job and they would not leave her alone.

Out of the blue came the offer for me – all expenses paid. It was a kind of miracle. If the Norwich day school would not mind cancelling my place with them ... It was a chance in a thousand. I was offered a scholarship that covered any costs involved, and I shall never understand why they wanted me – but first there was the interview. The school was not twenty miles distant, and you could come to it by bus. Father came with me. It seemed that it involved a written exam. I knew that I must uphold the honour of Marram Parish School, and I was like a foreigner in a strange world. It was a surprise that Father and I should be allowed to pass through the wrought-iron gates of Hale's School, Narborough. It was like as if I moved into a dream. This was a boarding-school. Miss Woodhouse had not been offended if I did not go to 'Norwich Day'. I thought of a boarding-school as something very desirable indeed, and I recalled all the school story-books I had ever read. There were 'japes in the dorm' and tuck-boxes and midnight feasts. Maybe they were such confidence tricks as Santa Claus.

The written exam over, I met the head, Mr. Hobbs, and the House Mistress of Byron's, which had been allocated to

43

the new intake of girls. Miss Huggard showed me the girls' uniform, and I thought it was wonderful. I thought that there was never such a fine school as Hale's, Narborough, and perhaps I was right.

I might have been happier in 'Norwich Day' and to sleep at home safe at night, but Mr. Hobbs had told me that I might come to Marram for a Saturday-Sunday break if the going got tough. In Hale's a lady took my measurements, and I understood why when parcels came by post with all my kit in about a week later. The next day a letter came from the school to say they had accepted me. I was to appear on such and such a date, with my trunk and tuck-box at the front porter's lodge, and then as an afterthought the trunk arrived by the carriers – it was big enough to take a body – with my initials painted in black on the side. So I was to forsake Mother and Father and Gran and Skippy and Marram and cleave to Hale's. I did not know what I was giving away – what I would miss so sorely.

I was delighted with life. I had seen the lacrosse court and now I saw 'the crosse' and the hockey stick. The uniform was all that I had imagined it to be. For summer there was a linen dress in light blue. In winter the same style in deeper blue wool. The hats were like boaters, straw in summer, felt in winter, and blue and white ribbons, that floated down to my waist, the shoes hand made by Thrussell's. This was the *dolce vita*.

At my interview, the Head had asked me about 'my swim'. They all did, or so it seemed. Mr. Hobbs had been interested to know how I had made it – what I had thought about.

"I was frightened most of the time. Then I thought of

'Eternal Father, strong to save' that we sing for the crew. It worked."

He asked me if I knew that the Parish was going to put up six sets of steps along the coast where there were none, and I was very pleased.

"It's amazing the strength of publicity, but don't be disappointed when the first big storm takes them back out to sea."

"The Marram dogs will be safe," I said. "For all time." For I thought he was joking about the sea.

"You don't believe me, Miss Rudd?" he asked. "Don't you put a limit on time?"

"The Lifeboat Institute set no limit on anything," I said. "Nor yet on giving. There are fifteen men standing by on each launching, when a crew of seven is all that's wanted. It's a kind of big honour to crew the boat. It was even a small honour for me that I was there to save Skippy ..."

"Ah, yes. There's the R.N.L.I. You confirm every ideal I've formed about you. The sea's got into your blood, and you've a tradition. We'd be glad to have you in Byron House."

We had gone into the details. It was all highly experimental. Hale's had always been a school for boys, one of the finest in the land. They would have to find how girls fitted in. The government had more or less insisted on woman's equality, and they would be watching us ... They had provided funds for the building of Byron House, and it more or less fitted in with the landscape. The spartan air of the houses was changing. They had even given up the refectory and its oak tables for the cafeteria system a few years ago. Things were no longer what they used to be – but there was no point in 'doing a Canute' ...

I had no idea what he was talking about, but then quite
suddenly I was there, getting a lift to Hale's with all my
luggage and with Father in the passenger seat in Robert
Penn's Sports Daimler. Father had wanted to travel by bus,
but Robert Penn explained that it just would not do.

'Else I'll take the old van," argued Father.

"Good God!" exclaimed Robert Penn. "Don't you know
that the place will be full of Jaguars and Rolls Royces. My
Daimler Sports has a panache about it, for all that it's
worth about a hundred pounds. Don't let Copper go in out
of depth any more, Rudd. I know what it's like to go to
boarding-school for the first time."

I went with no care in the world. We sped through the
wrought-iron gates, and I had no tears for Flint Cottage. I
realised that Gran was in the doldrums, but she often was.
Mother was too busy in the shop to do more than kiss me
good-bye and hurry back to work. We sped under an
avenue of trees, and then we were getting out at Byron
House and the hall porter was seeing to the luggage.

"Does your Father not want to see the matron then?" he
said.

I shook my head, and Father said he had better say good-
bye and go. The place was jam-packed with rich-looking
cars, but maybe the Daimler took pride of place. Robert
Penn held my hand in his.

"They say you can come home for a week-end
sometimes. I'll look forward to it."

"Thank you for bringing me," I said. "We never hang
about on railway platforms. Take care of Flint Cottage and
Skippy for me."

Father was getting into the car, and then they were gone. The porter took me up to see Miss Huggard, and she looked surprised to see me all on my own. She was very kind to me … took me to see my study-bedroom and the cafeteria.

"But we must insist that we still call it 'the refectory'. We have some meals here, but mostly we go to the big school refectory. It will seem very strange at first. I think that you must settle in and get your trunk unpacked. The girls are all arriving at once …"

I had never seen so many sad ladies and gentlemen putting on brave faces, nor so many girls. Everywhere I turned I came across little groups saying good-bye and no joy in them. I was feeling lost, so I set myself to do as I was told. In the boot-room I found my trunk, and I packed stuff into the tray of it and took it up flights of stairs to my study and arranged it tidily. It was all so brand new. My room was a square white painted box with a square window that looked out on trees. There was a bed that you made, and then slotted up and away slap bang, into the wall. The furniture was built in, even the writing-desk. You sat facing the wall and pulled down a flap and the desk appeared before you, and all the shelves for your papers. There was a basin with hot and cold, but it was cubicled into an alcove by a curtain. I went to the right side of the window and craned my head. I could see an open space and more expensive cars, and so many boys that I could not believe it, more parents too, and they were wandering all over the place like ants. There was no sign of the sea anywhere, but I had known we were well inland, yet I felt a sense of loneliness for the ocean.

There was a chair in the room with wood arm-rests and

another upright chair. I sat down and could think of nothing to do.

"Come down when the bell rings," Miss Huggard had said, so I just sat there and thought of Flint Cottage and wondered if the car had got safely home and if Gran was out of the doldrums. It was a long time before the bell went in a loud startling ring that repeated itself twice over.

I went out into the corridor, and there were girls there and they were unsure of themselves – all except one of them. She came out of the study next to mine and caught my eye.

"This is the end," she said. "It's what happens when you have the bad luck to pass exams. I'll never pass another as long as I live, so help me, God!"

She put out a hand and shook mine.

"I'm Mary Canning," she said. "Isn't this the most awful dump you ever saw? A social experiment, and I had to get caught up in it, a God-awful experiment with an establishment boys' school."

"I'm Hillary Rudd – study next door."

"What do they call you?"

I cast about for a name and knew that 'Little Fish' was not suitable any more and felt sorry that it was not.

"Copper."

"You're the sea-rescue girl. You've been on the box. Saw you. I'm glad to see you live. Let's go down to the refectory. They say it's terribly up-stage. We had caterpillars in the Brussells at my last place, and blancmange with lumps in it that you couldn't smash with a hammer. What matter, but the fees went up every year. Mother said she'd be bankrupt if I didn't pass for this hole. It's all on scholarship for us.

They said we're picked specially from England's best girls' schools. Ho! Ho! But I'd no choice. Mother's a widow and she's skint. Father's dead."

The refectory was really a cafeteria with a serving-counter and tables for four. Mary Canning was as cunning as a vixen, and she managed to get a good helping of the things we liked and refuse what we did not. She was well versed in the art of boarding-schools.

"It will be worse in the big school dining-room. We'll have some of the boys hating us and some after us like wolves!"

She was like a sprite of mischief. I was never to see her allow anybody or any circumstance to overcome her sense of clownish fun. She was to become my friend for life – to soar through one career after another and end at the top of her profession, but that was a long, long way ahead.

"My mother's an actress – one of the better ones. She says that the boys are furious that the government shoved us into Hale's, Narborough, especially because we had it for free."

Then there was the evening service in the School Chapel, and we girls up in the front pew, all dressed in identical uniforms, the hats with the blue and white ribbons, the blue and white striped blazers. The housemasters and the Head and Miss Violet Huggard sat in the Chancel at mahogany pews with candles in front of them in glass globes. The night coming dark. The boys thumped their way into the seats behind us, and I shall never forget that great roar of sound of the school hymn from so many voices. It was like the sea assaulting the shore. It was a gale-force tempest, and my heart was full of loneliness for Sea Lane, and the tears near enough to flow my eyes. They would be sitting down to supper in Flint Cottage. I was far out of my depth here. I would have crept like a snail into my shell only for Mary's elbow in my ribs.

"It's just homesickness, Copper. It gets better after a bit. Chapel is the devil the first night, always is, don't know why. I wish I didn't think of my ma all the time. She misses me. I'll bring some grub into our study later. We'll have a house-warming."

She knocked on my door in the late evening and brought a tin of sardines and two slices of cake. I shared my tuck-box with her, and we tried to make pretend that we did not both want home very badly.

"We'll get used to it. You'll see. It must be the devil for you if it's your first time to be a privileged child. That can be hell."

This was my first view into the rich man's world. It was a strange land. Mary said I was an inverted snob. There was nothing to fear. I would be taken at my face value, and already I had knocked up a good record. I was O.K. I had a future. I had only to put out my hand and take it. I only wanted to go home. In the nights I thought I should die of misery. I liked it in the classes. In a month Mary was accusing me of being a swot. I made a name for myself in the swimming-baths, after I overcame the difference between fresh and salt water. I had worried inwardly about my humble background. I was another 'Pip' in *Great Expectations*. I might call dumplings 'swimmers'. Why should I not? Hale's of Narborough polished a little of itself off on me. I began to watch my grammar. I began to take a pride in Bryon's. I learned that one did not lie, nor yet tell tales. In Hale's one corrected one's own work and allotted the marks due. One did not award 'extra plus', even with the certainty of not being found out.

Yet underneath it all I was hungry for the sound and the sight and the smell of Marram. I would even have relished the basement room, redolent of lobsters and bait and fish.

Then, after about four weeks, I was granted an exeat – thirty hours of break and a bus ticket, return to Marram. Indeed, I was just like Pip in Dickens's *Great Expectations*. I dressed myself very carefully in grey flannel skirt and white blouse, the school tie, the blue and white striped blazer. I tilted the boater over my eyes, and the blue and white ribbons were brave down my back.

I got off the bus at the stop and walked along the sandy road. I had caught an earlier bus and was not expected yet. There was nobody to meet me.

I had the ill-luck to run into Billy Grimes, the Butcher's son, out on a bicycle, delivering meat. He gave me a look of amazement and passed me by with no greeting, but had he not read *Great Expectations* too? In the Parochial School last term with Miss Woodhouse? Billy must have remembered Trabb's Boy. Billy doubled back to meet me up another lane, his cap off at the sight of me now and his face all amazement.

"Don't know yah!" he exclaimed. "Don't know yah!"

Again, he sped up one passage and down another and shot out into Sea Lane, just ahead of me, his cap in his hand again and himself bowing low.

"Pon my soul! Don't know yah! You're so proud grow'd."

I stood in his path and blocked his way, tilted the brim of

my boater more over my eyes, if that were possible. I gripped his handlebars, and made him prisoner. I gave him my monkey grin.

"Billy Grimes," I said, "I'm not proud grow'd and I never will be. If I were to tell you how I've missed you all you'd never believe it."

Then I took to my heels and left him standing, rushed on up Sea Lane and in past the clip-bell on the shop door ... seized Mother in my arms ... and all of us in Flint Cottage not far from tears ... only Gran, who was becalmed at the sight of me and pretending to have a fit of the doldrums, which she in no way had.

"Oh, Gran," I cried. "You're not in the doldrums! Surely the glass is rising and we have a fair wind today of all days. I've had a rough passage, but here I am, in port again. I've been thinking of you all the time, wanting to be home again."

She took me in from head to toe and said sourly that they'd maybe thought to make a silk purse out of a sow's ear.

"I don't rightly know if they haven't done it," she admitted. "Not that it were in any way necessary."

She cackled with laughter, her face lining into its familiar brown walnut.

I took her bony frame into my arms and knew it precious to me. Her face was tight close to mine, so that we could both hide emotions.

"There was no chance you'd ever come to be a silk purse, 'Little Fish', she said. "You're a lovely young lady grow'd, but there's no new loveliness about you. You've been a credit to us from the day you was born. Like the pussy cat,

52

you're fit to go up Lunnon to visit the Queen.''

Wild horses would never have dragged such words out of her, if I had not come to them so unexpectedly that day. She put me away from her after a bit.

"Sides, what you be wanting with a silk purse? You'll never want such a thing with that Penny Box Man on the mantelshelf. You're so taken with coming home that you never thought to take your burgling knife to that old fisherman friend of yours. I had him in my hand a time or two, when I were dusting, and he got so mighty heavy I could scarce find the strength to lift him. I think he's been putting by a fortun' for you.''

And indeed so he had, God bless him! So he had.

That was the start of twenty-nine hours of bliss. There was only one disappointment for me. In the afternoon I thought of the Martello Tower and my new grace and favour there. I said nothing, just that I must take Skippy for a walk on the beach. At the harbour I turned up the path to Robert Penn's place, for I wanted to see him again, though I was shy of him. He had been kind enough to give us a lift into school that first day. I had written to thank him and he had had a cake sent to me from a shop in Narborough. Narborough was a small country town near the school, and it had a prime tea-shop. I still had an adolescent passion for him, and at night I had dreams of him, so I walked with shyness that late afternoon, and I told the family nothing about it.

I went in by the gate, and Skippy was off like a rocket round the curve in the path to the door. I was surprised that Rouge did not bark. I was surprised when I saw the windows blind with shutters ... saw no flag flying ... saw the white notice on the shut door, a telephone number ... London ... and a long number. Robert Penn.

Nobody had told me he was away. I felt lonely all over again to see the place without life. Even the table and the iron seats and the boat things were locked into the shed. Skippy sniffed round all Rouge's tracks, and he was disappointed too. I ran back to the white gate and shut it carefully after me. Then I went to the harbour, talked to some of the fishermen, and they were all glad to see me again. The speed-craft was gone from its anchorage.

"He's up Lunnon, the Commander, you know, Mr. Penn, of the Tower. You've likely found his place shut. Poor gentleman! His mother were took real bad. He had to goo to her, smartish, up Lunnon, but he weren't in time. It's hard on him, because she were all he had. There will be lawyer's affairs to settle and that. He took that there red dog with him – one you saved from the tide. He said he'd be back soon's he could make it. He's a mighty lonely chap, but now he'll know what real loneliness is. We're keeping an eye on the Tower and seein' after his craft. It ain't right to see that flag not flying."

I ran along the sands to see the new steps, but they had not even started on them yet. It was a grey patch on the day. The fishermen hailed me as I went past on my way home.

"They're starting the steps Monday. Come back again whiles a month or two and the tides 'ont have had time to take 'em out."

One of them took off his cap and scratched his head.

"The place ain't the same wi'out Noah's little ole fish. Come back soon. Don't forget your old shipmates."

Foolish fond old men! I thought to myself, and I laughed at their folly, but the love was warm inside me for them.

"I'm a Marram mussel born, and I 'ont change. You'll never sell me off as a Whitstable Oyster, do you try ever so ha-ard," I said in my broadest 'Norfick'.

I went up the rise and back to Sea Lane, and there was such a tea laid for me.

Some time before supper when I was alone with Mother in the bake-house savouring the smell of the rich fruit cake, which was being cut for me to take back to school, I steered the conversation round to the Martello Tower.

"The men at the harbour told me Mr. Penn's mother was dead."

"Killed in an accident in Lunnon traffic," she told me. "Very sudden. He went straight away, but she had passed over. Did you know his father were lost off Malta in the war? Weren't only his mawther left. They were Naval folk, but you know that by the cut of his jib, that flag an' all. His mawther hated the sea after it took her man, settled in town, but it were cruel to her."

Mother was wrapping the cake up in grease-proof, and I knew there would be a feast tomorrow night.

"Mr. Penn," I murmured. "They call him 'the Commander' hereabouts."

"Our Mr. Penn had the rank of Commander," she said. "He's a real friend to us now because of your swim for Rouge. We've come to know him better. Invalided out of the Navy he was – broke his hip playing rugby – and he'd have gone far. His proper rank is Commander Retired, but he might have ended up a Admiral if he'd gone on, Pa says."

She laughed at me, told me that Mr. Penn 'had made a right fuss about' my steps.

"The Council wanted wood used ... cheap way of doing things ... but he called a meeting about it ... told them Marram should think shame of themselves, and it must be properly reinforced concrete or stone or nothing."

Father had come in to listen.

"He came out real strong," he said. "He said he'd put the steps up himself rather than let my girl get all snarled up in parish miserliness. It's the Commander's mawther's death had held it up. He had nobody left but her, and now he's got nobody. Your little ole steps was a blessing for him, for they'll take his mind off his sorrow. He's on now for a breakwater out to sea, to catch the force of tide. You should ha' heard what Parish Council had to say about that."

So this was the pattern of my home-coming. It was the only time that I did not find the Tower flag flying.

It was a sadness to say good-bye to Flint Cottage, but as the years passed it grew easier. Slowly and slowly, I drifted away from Marram. I loved Hale's. I became integrated with Narborough.

Then, when I had been a year and a term as a boarder at Byron's, I was sent for to go to the Head's study.

It was just before the Christmas holidays and spirits were running high. I searched my conscience to see if I could think of any cause for guilt. It did not seem so. Mr. Hobbs was in his Sherlock Holmes study, and he got to his feet as I knocked at his door and went in.

There was a legal-looking gentleman with him, black coat and striped trousers, a suave look about him and the appearance of having had too many rich sauces. His hands were plump and very white. Then I saw Father was there too, standing apologetically behind the door, with his seaman's cap in his hand.

"Father! Oh, Father! Why didn't you tell me you were coming to see me?"

Regardless of solemnity I flung myself into his arms and he held me closely to him and then put me aside, told me 'it were only some business to be done ... nothing to matter'.

Mr. Hobbs introduced Mr. Thomas Tulliver, of Jones, Jones, Jones, Tulliver and Jones, Attorneys at Law, Lincoln's Inn Fields, London. We all sat down, and Mr. Tulliver had set his card before me.

"It's all right, Little Fish. It's only some arrangements about your comin' to the school, more'n a year ago. We didn't tell you much about it. Reckon we all felt the Lifeboat Institute had most to do with it. Seems it weren't so, and now we're to know how it were."

Mr. Tulliver took over the conversation as we all sat down. He told us that these days most scholarships were state-provided, but mine was not. From the start I had been known as 'the R.N.L.I. Girl', for obvious reasons. I had won fame that had hit the media. Then followed a deal of stuff about the party of the first part and the party of the second part, and I was adrift. Then all at once Mr. Tulliver said to us that I had been handsomely provided for, but the whole deed had a Victorian flavour about it. The Royal National Lifeboat Institute had steered the course, but it did not put its hand in its pocket.

"A gentleman had come forward. He signed the cheque and will continue so to do, but he laid down conditions," Mr. Tulliver explained. "He's an eccentric in the world

57

today, in that he will accept no recognition – nor yet gratitude."

This eccentric benevolent gentleman reluctantly agreed that my family should know about it now, but he did not want publicity and he did not want gratitude. He did not want to be identified or sought after in any way, not under any conditions whatever. He would probably never find it necessary to make his identity known to me or my family. He had formed his own opinion of the youth of the present day, and then he had heard of this girl who caught the whole of England in her courage (This was me!!!) It was his wish that she be given the means to carry on to the top standard of education possible.

I understood some of it, but mostly I was 'mazed. It seemed that he had had qualms of conscience recently. I might get it into my head that he did not care about my welfare. With my parents' permission he wanted me to submit written reports to him, nothing too burdensome for the freedom of my life, just a formal letter to him, maybe once a term, reporting my progress. My parents might vet the reports if they wished, and he would not feel beholden to reply to me. He would have no gratitude expressed by me. He was adamant that he remained anonymous. His identity was not to be 'ferreted out'. I was to write a letter once every so often and to send it to him through the solicitors, who would forward it to him. It was very simple.

"It's a rum do," said Father. "I reckon a man should say thanks for the future that's been given his daughter."

"He says your father didn't ask for thanks, Mr. Rudd, nor yet your two uncles. It's not in the tradition."

"Tha's different," Father said awkwardly, and Mr.

Hobbs smiled at him and asked him if he knew the facts.

"It will never work," Father said. "Folk will talk."

"So we don't talk," Mr. Hobbs said. "Just among the family and no gossiping. This is to be a closed secret. I feel honoured to be included. It's just this conscientious man, who begins to think he should show an interest in what he's taken on. It's soon done. A letter once every so often and good work in school, good behaviour too. It's worked perfectly for a year and a term, and Miss Rudd is turned fifteen now. She's quite grown up."

He put his hands together, as if he prayed.

"If you want to know my opinion, and Mr. Tulliver could tell us if I'm right, but his lips are red-taped, this is some old gentleman who's lonely. I see him as a retired possible ship's captain who caught the news of the R.N.L.I. girl. He's maybe anchored in a London club, or by the sea in a cottage somewhere. There's been a change in his circumstances, so maybe somebody has died, maybe his heir. Suddenly, he's very lonely in the London club, and his youth gone, so he stretched for an ideal. Think of Pygmalion. Is it past him to have formed a plan to make Galatea, the perfect woman, having found the clay for the moulding?"

"You can't be meaning that serious, Mr. Hobbs," said Father, but he did not know Mr. Hobbs as I did. Mr. Hobbs smiled at Father and asked him why his daughter had not the ingredients for a perfect woman.

"By the Lord Harry! She's proved herself, Rudd."

"She were aimed for 'Norridge Day'," Father said defensively. "This here gentleman fired the cartridge for her to goo up the skies, like a rocket out at sea. It may be

59

that it's comfortable to be high in the sky, and we could never refuse her the chance. She's done well and her world will get to be a big ole place, but if she's happy, that matters. You gentlemen are all learned and I'm not, but I'm that grateful. I couldn't ha' done what's been done. If I can't say thank you, it's a rum do. Let it stand how it is, and I thank you gentlemen for your trouble. I'll see the lass writes her letters as this old feller wants. He must be a good man. That's for sure."

It was all Pip again in *Great Expectations*, and at least I could not suspect a Miss Havisham. This was a man from the start, and I knew of no convicts like Magwitch. My benefactor was the head of a board of R.N.L.I. somewhere, but he had personally picked up the cheques. It would be hard to write to a man with no face, and anyway perhaps I had imagined it all. I got a vision of a retired Admiral sitting in his London club scanning the *Telegraph*, to find out what ships were entering Liverpool, or Southampton or Port of London today.

The trouble was that I had to keep it secret except for the family. I longed to spill it all out in gossip to Mary Canning, who might have solved it at once.

As it was, Mr. Tulliver was fetched by his chauffeur in a black Mercedes, and Father and I were given an exeat for free passage in Narborough town for the afternoon, where we ate scrambled eggs and drank coffee – and worked through a plate of cakes.

Of course, we talked non-stop about the benefactor, and Father said 'he were a rare fine chap'. Somebody had said during the legal conversation in Mr. Hobbs's study that he was something to do with the sea, but retired. I had drawn up the picture of him at once, salted by the oceans of the world. He was my benefactor. Father kept impressing it on me that it was all top secret.

"Don't want to get all the folks in Marram spreading our private affairs round the *Eastern Daily Press*. I couldn't ha' set you up, not the way it's been done. Reckon best I can do is to see the Penny Box Man don't goo hungry."

"Maybe I'd prefer it that way," I said, and was sad when I saw him off on the bus and knew I must stay in Hale's.

"How can I write to a stranger?" I had asked Mr. Tulliver. His answer was terse enough.

"Think of your guardian as a naval man, as encrusted with the sea-salt as you are yourself. Gratitude can become a disease, the man said it to me himself!" Mr. Tulliver told me. "If she wants to become Copper Cinderella, let her pester me with gratitude and tricks of detection. The clock will strike midnight for her. Let her know it! The day she knows my identity and comes to me all softness, that will be the end of her story as far as I'm concerned, and that includes the settlement deed. She will be on her own. She can go to the devil or 'the Norwich Day', as far as I care about her."

They were hard honest words – meant what they said.

The end of the term was hilarious, but I was subdued. I had talked it all out with Father, and soon I would be home in Flint Cottage. At least we could all discuss it together then, but the days passed slowly. I tried to get the letter off to Lincoln's Inn Fields, and threw three drafts of it into my waste-paper basket as too banal for words. Banal was a new word, and I knew exactly what it meant by the time I had abandoned my letter to 'the benevolent old gentleman'.

Then came the day for going home. An urgent message
came for me by phone, and as I listened to it I looked
through the window and saw that the trees were being
battered by the storm. It was a full gale and the wind whined
through the window sashes and roared down the chimney.
The very last leaves were whirling in the quad like small lost
souls.

*Will you tell Miss Rudd that there's storm at sea and the
lifeboat's gone out. Her father won't be in Hale's to collect her as
usual, but Commander Penn will pick her up.*

So there was Robert Penn outside Byron's, and Rouge
giving me a welcome, my traps loaded in the jump-seat,
and Mary Canning flirting with the Commander, and then
we were away. We were too tough to put up the top, till the
rain-squall broke, yet we saw it coming.

"It's as rough as you like it at Marram, but there's no
panic. The boat's standing out towards a trawler in
distress. The R.A.F. has a Sea King helicopter on the
scene."

The flying twigs were slashing the screen, but then
suddenly we were out of the wood and the rain-squall on us.

We had the top up pronto and the car was a small safe
world.

"They'll be on the scene by now, Hillary. We'll stop at
the rise. The glasses are in the back somewhere." So was
Rouge. So were my trunk and all my traps. I rummaged
round the jump-seat till I found them, and then, after a
while, we ran up the hill and came out on the heights.

"Every time I see you, you've grown," he said. "Like
Trabb's boy, I don't know you today. You've grown up at
last, but thank God you haven't lost the monkey grin."

The skies opened in a hailstorm, but we were at the top of the rise. I had the manners to give him the glasses first. I could see the lifeboat near inshore, and the whirly bird hanging about in case ... The sea was almost impossible, but then nothing was impossible to Father – and Robert Penn thought I was grown up!

There was a cannonade of thunder, and Rouge must be comforted in the back.

" 'Eternal Father, strong to save', Copper. He's done it again, hasn't he. They're almost safe in the harbour, and soon you'll be safe home too. They'll be watching out for you at Flint Cottage. It's good to have somebody looking out for you. Let's take you home to them."

"Do you ever feel the great joy of a prayer answered, Mr. Penn?"

"Maybe."

"Gran must have known many unanswered, mustn't she? She's like the Rock of Ages. Yet I whittle about her leaving her teeth on the mangle, just because she's scared of the dentist and they don't fit. It's not that I'm all that brave about dentists myself."

He told me stop my 'whittling' forthwith. He had run Gran into Norwich a few weeks ago, and she had been fitted up with what she called 'a pair of teeth'.

"She even sleeps in them – likes the look of herself now ... If she were to be took sudden, she don't want to be took without 'em."

He put on that Norfolk inflection just for my benefit, because he teased me about it. "Whatever you do, tell her she looks great."

I sighed and lay back in the seat at his side.

63

"So now I have nothing left in the world to wish for. Father's safe and Gran has her teeth, and at any moment we'll see Flint Cottage and my folk. You were kind to bring the car. Soon I'll have my lucky Penny Box Man in my hand. We joke about him now, but the thought of the cottage and that chap on the mantelpiece sustains me through each term. All's well with the world. I'm glad that you've kinda become part of Flint Cottage too, since your mother ..."

In ten minutes everything was a bustle of welcome. Skippy was waiting with delight at the bottom of Sea Lane. Mother and Gran were at the door, and soon Father came riding up on his bicycle. They had taken five men off a Yarmouth trawler and seen the craft safe. The helicopter had picked up one of the crew from the sea.

It was so familiar with all the happy faces in the living-room and the table set with food and Mother running in and out every now and again when the shop-bell went. Mr. Penn and Father had a double ration of rum. When nobody was looking I lifted the Penny Box Man and he was very heavy. Gran looked like a duchess in her new teeth. Skippy and Rouge were asleep side by side before the blazing wood fire. Later on we were going to put up the Christmas tree, and Mr. Penn was gone, quite suddenly.

"See you around," he said, and I thought it might be a lonely thing for him, the Martello, with his mother not there.

He had taken himself away very casually, and I ran after him, jumped in the seat beside him and Skippy on my lap.

"See you as far as the main road," I said, and again I thanked him for helping me so much with school.

Hale's of Narborough

"You maybe steered me in the right direction, from that first day," I said suddenly. "Hale's was a different world from any I knew. I might have wandered there by bus in jeans and an anorak ... You knew there was a set of rules of do's and don'ts. You did it so tactfully and I do not remember saying thanks to you."

I was out of the car, and I realised that he was not my dream-lover any more. He had been superseded by a few film stars and about a dozen Hale's boys, who passed secret letters to me in the Chapel. It was the done thing ... It was all the stuff of innocent development towards adulthood. The Commander was my platonic friend now, and we talked about every subject under the sun. He would never know how I had once loved him. The thought was a little sad, but it was good to have a friend.

"Take care of yourself," I shouted at him, and the Hale's ribbons were waving in the gale. I had to hold the hat on my head as I grinned at him.

"Don't forget, I don't persecute trespassers any more," he said. "Don't grow up and leave me behind." And suddenly I knew tears in my eyes, and never realised what they meant.

65

3

THE LETTERS

I ran home up the Lane, and soon I was reverting to the true comfort of Marram Musseldom. Maybe I retained some of the polish that had brushed off from Hale's, but I sought suitable wear for the sea. It was a relief to put on the sail-cloth slacks that were a perfect washed-out blue, the white roll-top sweater, the anorak, ready to don when I went out, the Hale's head-scarf in school colours, sign of flying the colours in the home port.

I unpacked my kit and tidied everything away. My bedroom was a cabin, and Gran said it must be shipshape. All that was left was a box of note-paper that I had bought in Narborough for a Christmas present for the Martello Tower.

I decided to give Robert Penn the walking-stick instead. It came from Narborough too, just right, not even cut to length yet. It would make a suitable present for the Commander. Perhaps I have not even mentioned that he walked with a slight limp. I had a compulsion to write to my guardian – the writing-paper was superior to anything I had – and the walking-stick would be great for Robert

Penn, and at last I was going to be able to write a letter – perhaps.

Flint Cottage,
Marram.

Dear Mr. Nemo Blank, (This was Mr. Hobbs's suggestion)

I have just arrived home and want to write to you in the first happiness of this cottage. This is a signal from ships that pass in the night, perhaps never to know each other, but put like that, the mystery and romance are there. I accept your conditions and will obey your instructions, for I would never wish to displease you. So if it's formal, you must not know my emotions.

I am happy at Hale's. In Byron's House, they are determined to make us all into high-born ladies. The trouble is that I'm a Marram Mussel. We have deportment classes, things like walking with books on our heads, and elocution and how to curtsey. I ask you! Table manners are the same as we have at home. My Grandmother is worse than Hale's about standards. I have French and Latin and all sorts of luxuries, but Miss Woodhouse at 'Marram's Day' 'ad me gooing on all that ole rubbitch, and there's 'Norfick' for you.

One important thing is that we have French 'conversations' one afternoon each week in Hale's, when English is forbidden, and the attraction is that we have cream buns, at least two if we get through the first one quickly enough. There is a slight 'day at the races' about it. The French mistress wafflles round in high heels and a professional black gown, saying 'Doucement! Doucement! or maybe 'Lentement'. Sometimes she makes us do a penance by a Molière play in French. I think we might go down well on the stage 'up Lunnon', even if it wasn't supposed to be a laugh ...

But here is Marram and I feel the sea wash over my mussel shell and I come alive again, and today I look down at the waves a-roaring up the shore. The foam is flying high off the point and there are sleet showers. If you want more of me *'it's rum ole wather for the time of the year, bor', but I must stop pulling the dialect stop. It's just this cottage — and I wish I could have you see it, not only through my eyes. Let me tell you what it will be like tomorrow and the next day, but first, I have slacks and a sweater on again ... and sea-boots and an anorak standing by. If you want to see me, see me thus. Anorak in navy with scarlet hood lining, very faded blue jeans, a life-jacket if I'm going out with the fishing-boat, a monkey grin. This last I must mention. They say the Queen has one, so it pleases me if I have.*

Anyhow, come and look at Flint Cottage as it will be, these next few days. Christmas is on us — the big candle is burning in my window all the time, as dark falls soon. The fire in the living-room will blaze with the wood we collect all the year from the shore. Nobody returns from the foreshore without some driftwood. That's a house rule. The wood spits in the burning with the salt in it. It burns wet from the sea. Here we got 'suffin what's better'n gold' — and I promise to write English from now.

Anyhow downstairs for the run-up to Christmas there will be no time for writing letters. There are cakes to be iced and batches of doughnuts bobbing up in scalding fat. They must be pumped full of jam and set out on trays. The order list leaves one gasping, and Gran come to life again and is in there working like a teenager, but 'us young uns' never work like the old 'uns', do we? The oven pours out fresh bread to feed an army, for the holiday season. It looks enough to feed even the foreigners from as far as five miles off. The sticky buns are in demand. Everybody must have sticky buns, that come forth batch after batch from the oven, and we are all in good spirits. Father and Gran have tots of rum an odd while. 'Keeps Gran goo-ing,' says he.

It's best on Christmas Day. It has got stuck in time, this happy small unimportant place. The fishermen's families bring their Christmas dinners to cook in our ovens. I'm sorry but the ladies of the parish are called 'mawthers' and they bring the chicken or the pork or the duck or the turkey or the goose – the sacrifices to Christmas 'to goo' in the big oven. They are collected by their owners on to a piping hot dish with a spotless napkin to wrap them round. Our Christmas Tree is lighted, but we've not had time for it yet, only a glance. The presents are still unopened. The 'mawthers' are like anxious hens about the chicks, that have been roasted and they must get home. There's not one of them come to Flint Cottage with empty hands. They even put pennies in my Penny Box Man on the mantelpiece. We find things under the tree after it's over ... a hair ribbon for me ... a cod fresh from the sea, a lobster, a knitted shawl for Gran, a bottle or two of rum and this is treasure trove and maybe smuggled. That's the glory of it. It's opened and passed round. This is the true free Marram that I have learned to admire, that can cock a snook at the excise men – and he's likely there drinking level with the rest, like Nelson, telescope to blind eye. 'Brandy for the Parson, baccy for the Clerk'. I wish I had the library at Hale's for reference, but I recall the poem with 'Watch the wall, my darling, while the Gentlemen go by.' Then there are 'Five and twenty ponies trotting through the dark ...'

We have our own history of smuggling, and what seaman thinks smuggling a sin? They say that Sea Lane was the smugglers' route in the old days, but I have wandered away and must return to my cabin at the top of the cottage, which may have showed wreckers' lights in history, but I hope not.

I show a light every time the lifeboat's out to sea, when I'm home. Mother and I go up to the gap to watch for her safe return. You know my history. We're not high-up folks and maybe that's what you plan me to be, but I'm so proud of Adam, Seth and Joshua, past all education to be a high-born lady. This I tell you honestly, and it may cause you to cast me off, for my impertinence.

I have no pretensions to maritime matters. I started this report to you. I have run on and on, with nonsense. I think you will have torn the letter up and pitched it into the club fire, long minutes ago, turned back to the 'Telegraph' cross-word. I wish you could be with us this Christmas, with the company here, when the clock turns to the past again. I wish the ponies might come clip-clopping up Sea Lane and we could open the door to 'the benevolent gentleman', not to the smugglers. I hope I have not sickened you with 'Norfick' talk and marine matters. I must endeavour not to bore you, but I care. I'd like you never to have to know loneliness, unhappiness, nor yet neglect, only know that there is a small insignificant coble in the darkness, unknown or almost so. Call me in passing. There'll be a lantern ... This was supposed to be formal, but it has not worked out, has it? Gran would say it's a load of 'rubbitch', and mostly she's wise. I do not know how to sign myself ... only yours sincerely, Copper. Then I think that I have been wrong in not writing 'Hillary' for Hillary of the Lifeboat. Copper was just the name they put on me at Marram Parish School and it stuck, but should I settle for the dignity and honour of Hillary and miss the fun of Copper and the Butcher's son, Billy Grimes, who gave me the name at my school christening? Billy Grimes was Trabb's boy all over again, first day I came home from Hale's. He did that same running up and down back alleys, and when he confronted me, 'he didn't know me' and me fine in the blue and white ribbons of Hale's ... and I was so delighted to be home that I literally tilted my hat at him, and knew that if I travelled the world, I could never find a finer place than Marram.

I found Father and asked him if he wanted to see the letter, but he said it was a matter for myself. Mother was too busy with the shop, and Gran said she wasn't going to poke her nose into my affairs.

"That letter is confidential," she said. "You set it in the post box and send it on its way."

I zipped it in the pocket of my anorak and ran down the Lane with Skippy at my heels. Then I went on to the Post Office and pushed it in the main box. It might get off sooner. I thought of my benefactor in the club after Christmas and imagined him like an old weary Spencer Tracy. I pictured the letter arriving to him by the elderly waiter in the silent dignity of the smoking-room.

'*Dear Mr. Nemo Blank, I have just arrived home and wish to write to you in the first happiness of this cottage. This is a signal from a ship that passes in the night ...*'

I imagined that he might glance over the start of it and then throw it into the fire, reach for the port and look round for another mariner in the doldrums.

Anyhow, the letter was on its way. Then another sheet of biting hail came swirling down the road from the darkening sky. We turned into it, Skippy and I, and made for the sparking driftwood of the big hearth. It was past time we started on Christmas.

Next day, when the oven had been emptied of all its bounty and the people had taken their way home on Christmas day, we were alone as a family. It was then that we started to discuss this strange thing that had happened to us. We were not owing my fine future to the R.N.L.I. We had encountered a strange gentleman, called 'Mr. Nemo Blank'. I had written my letter to him ...

It was a matter between ourselves and there was no good spilling out our business to the whole parish. The lawyer man had made it quite clear to us, and we would abide by the gentleman's wishes.

Maybe we were a bit like the Cratchett family, in that we toasted Mr. Nemo Blank in a quartern of gin, and wished him well, except that we used rum.

We had a very merry Christmas, and I was fifteen turned. In the New Year, I went back to Hale's, and it was the Lent term – the worst term by far. I cheered myself by watching every post as it came, but nothing came from Lincoln's Inn Fields. At last I gave up hoping for an answer, and there was an empty feeling in the pit of my stomach. It was obvious that I was going to get no answer. He had objected to the foolish tone of my letter to him. He wanted nothing to do with a Marram Mussel, and I had been a dickey to write such stuff, and a dickey is Norfolk for donkey. It would have been better if I had addressed him as 'the party of the first part'.

Mother wrote to me regularly every Sunday. I answered every Wednesday. This was the total of my letters, in and out of Hale's. One of the girls came round to distribute the in-coming mail every day, and on the 25th January there was a strange letter addressed to Miss Hillary Rudd. It had been posted in London, W.1., the day before, First Class. The envelope was opulent-looking and square. Inside the sheets of writing-paper were deckled quarto. The signature was a squiggle, that was not to be deciphered. It started on the left and went across practically the whole width of the page and then plunged to the bottom of the sheet and disappeared. There was a fine arrogance about it.

Dear Copper,

Thank you for your letter. I must apologise that I did not answer it sooner, but it needed much thought on my part.

Maybe you will never understand what effect it had on me. You forced me to see this place called Marram. You set out your life in confidence, as if you stood in front of me and said 'see this, and see this'. You admitted me to Flint Cottage, and I thank 'ee.

Then I began to get doubts as to what I had done. Maybe I was wrong to think that I could improve on such a life.

I begin to pity you now under the pressures of Hale's. Who can ever say that you'd not have lived happily as you were? You might never move further than Sea Lane and be happy ever after.

Now I picture you unhappy, scraped out of your shell into a cruel hungry sea. I know myself guilty of interference. I had imagined you deserved a reward, the best the country could offer you. Maybe you possessed the best already.

I want you to give this some thought. Choose for yourself, if you want all this further education. Why should I force you into exile? Mr. Tulliver can prepare some gentler deed as your reward for gallantry.

As you are, maybe you'll settle for Flint Cottage ... be happier not to see what the outside world's made of.

My ideas for you might never work, yet I have your reports from Mr. Hobbs and he promises me that you will fulfil every hope we have of you. He promises you the earth, but perhaps it's the devil stealing Marram away from you. You might be happier messing about in boats, but Hale's is drawing visions of degrees and diplomas.

I quote Mr. Hobbs, when he said it would be criminal to deny you a 'crack' at the universities!

"She'll make it by her own efforts, this outstanding girl. I would not advise any change in plans at this stage. You'll shut out the bright promise she has ..."

Yet, if you might prefer to get back to that wonderful place you've shown me in your writing, you're a free agent.

Happiness is the thing, and there's such happiness at Marram, even if maybe the world's shut out.

I want you to think it out and make up your mind. You will not lose financially by it. Mr. Tulliver will see to that for me. Maybe it is just because I had never known such a place existed as Flint Cottage. If you passed it by in Sea Lane, you might never know anything but the fact that it used to be a coast-guard station.

I will be happy if you agree to carry on as we planned, but I in no way enforce it. Just give living a chance to let you see what else it could be ...   *Sincerely yours,*

Squiggle, Squiggle.

Almost he signed himself and then went back to the squiggle.

He typed my name and address, and his typist should have cleaned her machine. It was writing with an inked 'u' in Rudd, so that it read more like Rodd – and it was a strange missive indeed.

He was a perfectionist and his conscience niggled him sorely. I had sold him Christmas at Marram and he did not know that I was very happy in Hale's.

My letter went back to him by return, for I knew how one dreads an error of judgement in case it causes unhappiness.

Byron's House,
Hale's
Narborough.

Dear Mr. Nemo Blank,

I was excited to get your first letter, but worry that I have caused you worry. I assure you that I am perfectly happy and could wish for nothing more. I thought about all you said and I know that being here makes home seem all the better. Being at home, I look forward to school again. There is such a spirit in Byron's. I think we imagine ourselves as leaders of Woman's Lib. The fact that we were the first girls admitted to such a famous boys' school puts us on our mettle. I just cannot explain the sheer fun we have. Here is a beginning to something that will go on. The boys accept us now, and there is a very healthy competition between the other houses and Byron's. I still cannot grow accustomed to the great roar of voices at chapel when three hundred boys sing. Byron's has a special rôle to carry out. We have to let it be seen that girls in school may upgrade the standard. We have to see that we're a good influence, and I think we are. It's a difficult path to walk, so that we're not thought 'prissy'. It's akin to the day I bloodied Billy Grimes, the Butcher's son, in Marram's Parish School. Maybe I have the feeling of carrying some flag or another ... and Billy is gone to 'Norridge Day' and will soon be serving behind the counter, in his father's shop. Poor Trabb's boy! Poor Trabb's boy!

I know there are unseen things for my future, I know that you've opened the door for me to step out. I don't want to be narrowed down to having a mind that stops learning off short at sixteen. God forgive me for confessing I'm a snob. I don't want to spend my life selling sausages in Mr. Grimes' shop. This is a secret mean thought. I believe I may have started to confessing thoughts that should not be said, but it seems as if I confess them to a field of standing wheat. 'The king has asses' ears, asses' ears, asses' ears.'

It is such a comfortable thing to have somebody who will know what I mean. Let me stay at your feet and see if I can prove myself worthy of your kindness.

As the months passed, as the years passed, maybe I told my story to the standing wheat. I told it all.

'The king has asses' ears, asses' ears, asses' ears ..."' I made no effort to identify him. There was such orderliness about it. School went on and our letters flowed back and forth like the tide. Maybe I used him as my diary. All my small doubts and fears were there. No person could have enjoyed such confidence. I came to him for advice. I came to him for comfort. He learned all about me, but I learned nothing about him, and the years ran out like sand through a glass.

I knew about Robert Penn suddenly, surprisingly. I was in the bookshop in Narborough and I came on a stand of new novels by Robert Penn, just published. I picked up the top book and looked at the wave that swept the dust-cover. I turned to the back and cover, recognised the Martello Tower and Robert Penn's photograph. I must have stood with my mouth agape ... 'Famous for his books of the sea, Robert Penn had won fame across the whole world ... ex-naval officer, his Father lost in the Mediterranean in the Second World War.

'Robert Penn is an expert on maritime affairs and writes about things that maybe he has lived.'

"Oh that," he said, when I challenged him with my discovery. "I thought you knew all about it. You must have seen me at the machine in my study on the top deck. Did you think I was writing letters? All day writing letters? Good God! I do crime stuff, too. It's far more popular with the public – the very poor man's Sherlock Holmes – that's me!"

Fifteen to sixteen, sixteen to seventeen, seventeen to eighteen, and I had collected a sheaf of what Gran called 'sustificates' to set on her lap.

"There's the sum of my harvest, Gran. They don't look much, but if I slit them into a government slot a university education will come out, gratis and for nothing … only that our benefactor is not willing to have things done like that. He wants to keep it on just the same way, so maybe I'm still to keep my 'Daddy Long Legs' and perhaps I have grown to love him …"

The years had run so smoothly away, but they were gone and I had to start at the beginning all over again.

All the time, I had spent my holidays at Marram, and I was skilled in the art of sending Robert Penn's speed-bird leaping from one wave-crest to the next across a choppy sea. Usually he fetched me from Hale's, and even if he did not I would no sooner arrive at the cottage than I would change into sea-going gear and run off down the path to the Martello Tower. He would be writing as usual, scribbling on a jotter or typing. He had a section high up in the Tower that he kept for writing only. It had a window that commanded the North Sea. The walls were lined with reference books, and there were stacks of typing-paper and a box of carbons and folders. When I showed an interest in his writing, he steered me away from it. It seemed to be a very private subject that he had no wish to share with me. It was easy enough to lure him out to the speed-bird. I had developed a fine skill with it. I could take it inshore, right slap-bang into a sharp edge of rock I knew. Then when there was no hope of escape I was able to sheer off six inches of disaster, and go full speed to sea again. I never scared him. Always he laughed and gripped his pipe between his teeth.

"You'll do that once too aften, Copper. Don't forget

you'll be in here, beside me. It's cold and it's deep at that particular place, and if you're fooling round with a car at the cliff that begins on my front door, make sure your brakes are holding. This spot you choose for aquatic skill happens to be what I call 'a drowning hole ...' "

He raised a brow at me.

"I don't want to lose the car too. If you're monkeying about with the car and it's parked near the dip, *reverse* if you value your life."

Maybe I thought of him as the brother I never had. Hale's had been a great breeding-ground for romance. We had integrated with the boys in dramatic society, dances, debates. Mary Canning and I had had a choice of what we called 'lovers', but they would never have fitted into that category. They were butterflies and maybe lasted a few sweet weeks. Then there was another butterfly – and another. There was a great passing of love-letters in Chapel, God help us. Out in the fishing-boat with Father and Billy Grimes, I would catch Robert's eye on me.

"I'm just 'sat here' waiting for you to grow up," he'd say.

I am glad now that I never told him that he was too old. I had got accustomed to very young youth at Hale's. It was Gran who put me right about that.

"Robert Penn don't draw the pension yet, lass. *There's* a man that could measure up to any of your young gents in that fine school, where you got they 'sustificates' of yours. The Penns have always had winter in their hair. His grandpa were silver 'fore he were half-way to thirty' – his paw just the same. It's bred in them. Robert Penn's children will have the same silver touch to their heads."

She looked at me over the top of her glasses like the old

advertisement for Mazawattee Tea, and I turned my back on her and watched three children on their way up Sea Lane to the dunes.

"I'll never wed, Gran. I'm a career woman."

"Is that so?" she asked acidly.

"Robert Penn's the brother I never had," I explained. "There's no more to it than that."

I could feel her eyes like gimlets in the small of my back.

"Then it's a funny thing the way you're not home five minutes, but you're off to the Tower to see that brother of yours. Have you ever thought of the day the Commander will find a bride? There'll be no more dashing off to his fine house then. His wife 'ont approve of having you under her feet all day!"

I thought it was time I changed the subject. I knew by this that Robert Penn was Gran's white-headed boy, just because he had fixed up her dental problem.

"Gran, you must be the first to know. I showed you all those certificates. They've offered me a place at Wentbridge University. I have to go there next week for an interview."

I received by post all the arrangements for my journey to Wentbridge and my benefactor's felicitations at my results. Mr. Tulliver was to collect me off the Wentbridge train, for there was a new legal arrangement to be drawn up. My benefactor did not want one item changed, I could cast my certificates to the devil for all he cared. He would not allow modern pressures to be put on me. Education must never be by treadmill. I would have time to enjoy this ancient university as it had been long ago, when Edward was king.

This was the first time he revealed a part of himself. He had planned to meet me himself, and then at the last minute he had found he would be out of town. Mr. Tulliver must represent him and would collect me from the long platform that he knew so well.

This was the first hint he had made of his identity. Almost he had met me. Then he had drawn back. He was a graduate of Wentbridge then? In the time of King Teddy? Surely not. He knew my college. He might finally have wanted to see the girl he was backing, but he had stopped up short. King Edward, the Duke of Windsor? was he Wentbridge ... but King Teddy was!

Father might have accompanied me. Mother did not want to go. Gran was not quite up to it. At the end, they all bowed out, shy of the fine grandeur of the establishment.

Robert Penn made no mention of it, but he watched my every move. He seemed very much on edge. Told me I was setting out into a jungle of tigers ... and was unhappy in saying good-bye.

I arrived at Wentbridge long station on the early train and was glad to see Mr. Tulliver waiting. He had his long black car, and it ferried us about, and the chauffeur did not care a jot for the traffic.

It was all very calm and orderly. First, there was my Lady Tutor to see. Then we were gliding through the traffic to the Via Devana. Here was the university lodging house I was to share with Mary Canning. It was a three-storied Victorian house, and Mary Canning was to room here too. Somebody had gone to great pains to make the way smooth for both of us.

Mary's luggage lay in the hall. Mr. and Mrs. Willson hovered. There was a breakfast waiting for Mr. Tulliver and me. The snow-white cloth and the fine English breakfast of bacon and eggs, served as it had been served in King Teddy's time. The silver shone, the china glistened, the table-napkins were shaped like bishop's mitres and laundered fresh every day.

"We're that glad to meet you, Miss Rudd," the Willsons said. "It's not often we get a celebrity 'at ours', but we saw you on the television. That were a rare fine thing you did. Are they still alive, the little old dogs. Reckon they owe their lives to you."

"Skippy's a very old gentleman now."

We dined in a hotel by the river, after I had signed a sheaf of legal documents in my new sitting-room.

The hotel was sheer Wentbridge, with the dining-room over-looking the river, and punts going up and down disturbing the mallards. We drove through the city, and Mr. Tulliver gave me a run round the colleges.

The shops were splendid caves of emeralds and diamonds and gold moidores for the foreign tourists.

We had finished all our business by mid-afternoon, so we took tea at the Copper Kettle, and Mr. Tulliver saw me off on the train to the coast by five-thirty.

He stood at the carriage window as the train moved off.

"I'm glad it's to run as before. It's been a great success. I'm starting you out on a career tonight on the greatest adventure of them all."

"But Peter Pan had it that death was the greatest adventure," I objected, and maybe he did not hear me, for the train was gone and I was away – and the platform was empty. It was time for me to settle down in my carriage for the East Coast – not Marram, but the nearest station to it, and maybe Father in the van to meet me.

The Letters

I was to share the rooms with Mary Canning. I had been feeling very much a new girl, and suddenly it might have been Hale's all over again that first day. I did not have to ask who had made the wheels turn so smoothly. My benefactor had willed that my education proceed in just the same way. Mr. Tulliver said that my benefactor was a man who at one time had almost lost the will to live. Perhaps I had given it back to him. I still had no more idea who he was.

Maybe he still sat in that club and waited to hear from me. I had written so many words to him and we were trusted friends now. He was very pleased with the way I had conducted his experiment. Wild horses would draw nothing further out of the legal gentleman, but he admitted that I had done extremely well.

"You'll have to pay attention to the traffic," Mr. Tulliver had warned me. "The usual transport to and from lectures is by bicycle. You must provide yourself with one. The college porter will tell you where to go. See that you purchase a padlock for the wheel too and paint your college number on your rear mudguard in white. There is a regrettable number of bicycles 'borrowed' with no permission when a student's late for lectures. I'm glad to know that it's all to run as before – this education of yours. It seems that you have brought sunshine, wherever you went. I feel that I am starting you out on a great adventure today."

It ran through my head in remembered sentences all the way to the junction for Marram, and there was Father in the navy blue van, waiting to meet me.

4

THE NINE-PIN TRAGEDY

Then, suddenly, all the preliminaries were over. I had landed with my trunk and my hockey-stick and my crosse at the university lodging house in the Via Devana. Right on my heels came Mary Canning, sparkling over like a bottle of pop.

"Suddenly we're free," she cried, and started straight into the business of unpacking and making herself at home. From time to time she put her head in through my door and went on with the conversation.

"There's a different climate here. In Hale's, there was always somebody breathing down our necks. Now we can do what we like and go to the devil, if we please. It's up to us to make our own way. It's tricky for starters. There's always a bill to pay. I propose to play it cool."

Mary had been studying form as well as mixing metaphors. She came in with a cup of coffee in each hand and a tin of biscuits under her arm, sat herself down.

"There's an advantage in being ex Hale's, Narborough. Dozens of our chaps have come up."

This must surely be her usual exaggeration, and I smiled at her. "Peter Cunningham is for King's, and Ellis Minor is for Downing. Ellis Major, elder brother, took his degree here. He's a house officer in the hospital," I said.

"We're not strangers in a strange land, Copper. We'll soon find out what goes on. Everybody I've met so far tells me to get a bicycle, soon as I can, paint my number in white on the rear mudguard and watch I don't get it pinched."

People had been advising me to be careful in the traffic. It came to a halt at rush hours and between lectures. A car was less than useless, so everybody rode a bike. I had seen them in stacks parked all over the place, and knew that the police had a sale of stolen or maybe of 'borrowed' cycles at intervals.

We talked till our throats were hoarse, and then got on with the turning of our two pairs of rooms into 'home'.

She and I were for the same girls' college across the road. We braved the steady flow of traffic and did a tour of the whole place. Then we came back to Mrs. Willson's for high tea, because we wanted to explore the town. Mary had the whole situation cased. The food in college was 'prime'. The University had many houses, and each with a chef. We dined in our college at an old refectory table every night, and they kept standards as high as times allowed – which was bloody high.

"This is to be the best part of our whole lives," Mary said. "A time we will remember for always. Now it begins and let's taste the whole of it. Let's not waste a moment ..."

We planned to walk down the hill and slap-bang through this university city, and so we did. There would be no time tomorrow. We were due to report to College early on. We had a super time, and when I came home I sat down and wrote to my Guardian – but first I wrote a letter home. When the letters were done, I walked along the path and posted them.

The Nine-pin Tragedy

My dear Guardian,

I have settled in safely and Mary is with me, as you know, and we are both very, very new girls. The lodgings are grand and most comfortable and Mr. and Mrs. Willson do not seem to realise that standards of living have changed since the First World War – that means it's super.

I must tell you how we explored the city. You will probably know the place well. We went straight down the hill. I think it may be the only hill in this flat land. Across a bridge, the full moon came out from behind the clouds and showed us one silvered silhouette of beauty after another – the colleges behind the walls of history. Here was the heraldry of the front gates. One after another they paraded for us with haughty majesty. We spoke about all the great names. We stood and stared. We belonged.

Back to more mundane things, we surveyed the windows of bookshops, and this was in a place where the shops almost met across the street at roof-level to shake hands. There were chop-houses and coffee-houses. Further on, we recognised the wide parade and the most famous chapel of them all, and I thought of Peter Cunningham and how he would attend service here. We had been friendly in Hale's, and it was he who had been the first boy in Hale's to pass a letter to me. I wonder if he will ignore me in Wentbridge. He is to read medicine too, as you know I am. His father is a doctor, so Peter has lived with the experience of a G.P. household.

After a while, we saw a bus going to the hospital and we took it. The Complex is on the very edge of the city. The University is a place of historic grandeur. It has been here for so long. The hospital is a city in a city and at night it looked like a thousand liners all lit up like some great fleet with square ports. This is where we will work, if we are lucky with exams. Mary and I both took to Science at Hale's, as you know. You said if I wanted to be a round peg in a round hole, medicine was for me. Walking about a tenth of the hospital, for it is huge, I thought I could dream the future. Maybe I did. If I'm to be a doctor, here is the place to learn how. It is an awesome place, the best of the modern world of science, just as the colleges are the best of the past, but then some of the colleges are very new too, and I am teaching my grandmother to suck eggs.

Mrs. Willson brought us to earth when we got back to our rooms. She was glad to hear we had been to the hospital. It would be a comfort to have two medical students, especially 'lady doctors'!!! She suffered cruel with her back and was always having to go to Out-patients, though the doctors said there was nothing wrong with her except overweight. In future, we might be able to help her with advice.

We looked at her dubiously, but she was serious.

"Now off to bed, like two good girls! You have a busy day tomorrow, and breakfast will be on the table nice and early and I'll expect to find everything enjoyed and clean plates after you."

That was the start of what I considered the best part of my life, but maybe I was very wrong. If I take an inventory of the years, maybe Marram was better. There was a special quality of peace that Marram had, where the worst thing that could happen was Billy Grimes putting sour milk in my hair and baptising me after a genus of snake.

Wentbridge was splendid, but it had pressures. It was all training and steeplechase. If you neglected your work, it could creep up and strike like any copper-head.

The next day we started on the routine we were to know so well. As Mary said, we had nobody breathing down our necks. We were to meet opposition, against far brighter students than ourselves. We soon found it better to attempt a maximum effort, but there were diversionary activities too. It was an attractive playground and we made the most of it. We gravitated to many of our old friends from Hale's. We made many new ones. We fitted our work-play ratio to Hale's ideals, and so we passed the first three years, and there would be little point in describing it in detail. It has nothing to do with this story, or almost nothing, for maybe it came to nothing for me ... like sand running out of my hand.

Then it was time to turn to the Hospital Complex and come to meet actual patients. Ellis Major had entertained us in his rooms there, and we had been associated with some lectures and preliminary meetings, minor practical stuff. Peter Cunningham and I were still very good friends. We moved round in a select Hale's clique, mainly medicals. I think Ellis Major had a good influence on us, for he was determined that his young brother would work, and he included the rest of us in his flock.

See me then at the beginning of the Long Vac at the end of my third year, sitting in my rooms, writing to my Guardian.

> *Via Devana,*
> *Wentbridge.*

Dear Penny Box Man,

Please accept the title, which is 'hon' I think. I consider 'Nemo Blank' too cold and austere, for what you have become. You know I left the Penny Box Man in Marram, because it is a boisterous place here on occasion. I knew he was too fragile for happiness away from home. Then I missed him, and I was impertinent to make you a locum tenens. Once he gave me a fraction of the important things you give me now. A three-penny bit sustained me and brought me great happiness in the old days. You have seen to the smooth run of my life. Never have I repaid either of you. I am hoping this is not an 'avaricious' name to

89

bestow. It's an old and tried affection.

I have got the exam results and they are answered prayers. Next academic year, October, I come to the crunch in medicine, I move into residence in the Complex. Meanwhile celebrations are overwhelming the University. Mary and I and Peter and some others are planning breakfast on the river after a night at King's Ball, but thought we'd improve on the usual form. We pushed back the years and hope it keeps fine for us. There are nine of us on a glorious adventure — four ladies and five gentlemen. I wish you could see us. The men are to be in drain-pipe trousers and top hats — with the hats too tall. It is impossible to describe the high-fashion of Mary and me, not to mention Susan and Elizabeth in our leg-o'-mutton sleeves, mounted on iron horses, these bicycles, all ex-vintage district-nurses'. Peter has a genuine penny-farthing. The other boys have old iron horses with a bar in the middle and they're just right. Mr. Willson is a Fen man and he went out into this antique land and came back in a lorry called 'Here Comes Papworth' with the job lot of bicycles.

So we will go to the ball first and then set off along the country road before break of day for the hotel lawn by the river, a few miles. I hope Peter does not break his neck off the penny-farthing.

Maybe I should try to describe the ladies' dresses. We all chose pastel colours, rose and blue and lavender and apple-green. Our skirts sweep the ground and the sleeves are Edwardian and the waists very small indeed. The 'bodices' are high in the neck with a row of tiny buttons. We have pill-box hats with veils ... white gloves. First the glamour of the ball. Then a clear night and that small country road, and after breakfast the trip home to Wentbridge. It is happiness almost not to bear.

I should have given you a detailed list of my marks, but this enthusiasm for the whirl of society has blotted all the sense out of my head. Also I have been afraid that I identified you as Penny Box

Man, Mark Two. How could you be anybody else? The Money Box was the high spot of my baby days. Why should you not have the decisions about my adult years ... and that's unfair on Flint Cottage ... and in October, I will be walking the wards, being very sorry for the poor old patients who creep like old grey rats along the eternal corridors and know themselves mortal, waiting for the sign, 'thumbs' up or 'thumbs' down. We had a dress rehearsal tonight for tomorrow, and I wish you could have been here. The Willson's are enthusiastic, and we would have never got the pattern of the dresses, never fitted the sleeves without Mrs. Willson. The men are all elegant, and so are we. The skirts are enormous and have dress guards on the mudguards. It is like Arcady tonight with the long summer light and no sign of rain for tomorrow or the next day. I have fallen in love with the idea of giving you the name in my heart. Dear Mr. Penny Box Man, forgive me all my follies and grant me this indulgence ...

I signed it 'with love from Copper' and ran off to pop it in the post, and tomorrow was Midsummer's Day when anything could happen.

It seemed as if it might never come, but it did. Midsummer evening, the darkening air seemed filled with electricity, but there was hardly any darkness all night, only the music and the dancing and the dawning. The sun was lightening the eastern sky when we reached the village. I remember the table set out for breakfast, the goblets of grapefruit, the plates of eggs and crisp bacon, the cups of hot strong tea and the punts on the river ... and French croissants, and crisp toast and home-cooked marmalade. The ball was over. The night might have been spent in Arden for the mood that had taken us. In an interval, while he held my hand, Peter had asked me to marry him. It was all fixed in his mind. His parents liked me. They would welcome me into the family. There was a place for me in a dynasty of doctors. Peter would never love anybody else. He had made up his mind as far back as the first time he saw me in the Chapel at Hale's.

It is strange that I had never carried the thought of Peter Cunningham along to its logical conclusion. He was everything I admired in a man. We had kissed and caressed and taken it all for granted, nothing more, nothing less, yet this morning was perfection.

"It's a very serious decision, Peter. We must think about it," I whispered.

"We've had years to think about it," he laughed.

Then somebody said that it was time we were starting back for Wentbridge, and the idyll was interrupted.

We all stood by the garden gate with our bicycles, and the wind shivered my spine. I took Peter's hand in mine and would have been content to stay there all my life.

It was like the morning of the world. Never could there have been such air. It was just three to four miles back to the Via Devana. Then it would be time to load my kit into Robert Penn's new vintage car and steer for the sea and Flint Cottage.

It was a narrow country road with high summer hedges. We rode two abreast, our lady dresses blown blossoms on the brightness. I think that not one of us had ever been happier. The exams were past and conquered, and we could look forward to long laziness and total relaxation. Then in October we were ready to face fresh challenge with all the excitement of the last Medical School years.

There were nine of us, all told, five old Halesians and

four guests. Nine – that's what put the name on it! The Nine-Pin Tragedy.

While we had breakfasted, there had been a Juggernaut lorry on its way towards Wentbridge, making for Harwich and the Continent. The driver had come from Liverpool and perhaps it was time he rested. He came on us round a corner, and I wonder what he made of us, riding along in our Edwardian gear. Peter and I came first. We went two by two, and all about us was sunshine and dawning and youth. Perhaps we were singing. We were certainly smiling. The dresses would have shone their colours like a summer's garden – green, blue, pink, lavender.

It was done between one minute and another. There was no time to grasp the finality of it. Yet time slowed down too and every slightest movement was deliberate.

The rear off-wheel of the lorry was as big as such wheels are. It had been coming loose, and now it worked free and came rolling along the road. There was no stopping it, no diverting it. It seemed to move with a fearful slowness and deliberation. We came straight into its path. For all the slowness, there was no time.

It sent us flying to right and left. It scattered us about the road like small bright-coloured marionettes. We lay in grotesque poses, with no order about us, sad foolish little bundles of clothes.

The driver could not comprehend what had happened. He jumped down out of his cab and scrambled back through the hedge and came walking stiffly along the road. His eyes fixed on the great tyre where it had juddered to a halt against the last of the cyclists.

First of all, he came on a girl and a boy, still hand-in-hand. The boy had hair that shone fair in the sun, but there was no doubt he was dead. There could be no surviving such a mortal blow. The girl was a copper-haired doll that some spiteful child had taken by the legs and beaten against the nursery dresser. She was a broken doll.

Vaguely he wondered what he had done and who they were – like members of a concert party at the seaside. 'Humpty Dumpty', he thought. 'Humpty Dumpty.' The wheel had broken 'Humpty Dumpty', and all the king's horses and all the king's men could never put Humpty Dumpty together again.

In his mind had been a suspicion that the off rear was faulty. He had intended to stop, and look at it and then the city was in sight ...

There was a woman coming out of a cottage door, her face as white as chalk.

She walked round the fallen bodies, felt a hand here and straightened a crooked limb there, tucked a towel against a bloodied chest.

There was terror in her face as she looked back at him.

"I think they're all dead, mate," she said. "Us had better fetch help quick. There's a phone at mine."

I could know nothing of this. I was beyond all knowing. The evidence was all to come out at the inquests, how Mrs. Wolfe had sent for the ambulances and the law. First of all, she had seen that the lorry-driver was not badly hurt, only shocked. After all, the lorry had careered through the hedge and was lying in White's Meadow. He had just scrambled through the hedge, and he was scratched by wild-rose thorns. It was all in the *Wentbridge Daily News*, and the cottage lady had given evidence.

94

"I saw it happen," she said. "There was nobody at fault. The tanker shed its wheel, and that there wheel came on down the road with a humming sound, like a child's top might have sound. The lorry were through the hedge into the meadow. There was a smash-tinkle-tinkle, and then the man clawed his way back. That wheel were as straight flung as a nine-pin. They was riding their bikes on the correct side of the road, two and two. They were skittered round the road like nine-pins – but it were pure accident. We did what we could, Mr. Atkinson, the driver, and me – got help. They had three ambulances and a fire engine and Police Accident lights set up. The road were closed to traffic a long time."

The coroner thanked her, and Mr. Atkinson's legal man thanked her for the help she had given at the scene of the accident. The Coroner said she was a very good witness and had been the right person in the right spot. The papers were full of it for a long, long time. Rose-pink, blue, green and lavender, the colours of the dresses and the leg-o'-mutton sleeves. If they said it once, they said it a dozen times, as they tried to put Humpty Dumpty together again.

There must have been nine families, the morning of the accident, maybe expecting their children home later in the day, not knowing that the wheels of tragedy had started. It was inevitable that soon the telephone would ring or maybe a policeman's hand knock at the front door.

"Mrs. Cunningham, do you think I might speak with the doctor, please? It's a personal matter, not to do with the practice. No, I'd better speak with him first."

In the Casualty Department at Wentbridge, Operation Nine-Pin Tragedy was being set up. The wailing of the ambulances had come and gone. Extra staff had been draughted on duty. The Sister-in-charge was making a survey of the multiple accident. She was accustomed to a driver's shock and the way he talked out his horror.

"Jesus, Sister! I didn't mean to do it. They were just like kids after a party, like dolls flung all over the road. I thought that wheel weren't right and I'd been meaning to have a look at it. I took the wrong turn in Wentbridge. Next minute, the wheel rolled past me and the lorry were in the meadow. Are the kids hurt bad? If they are, I'm to blame. I ought to have seen to that wheel."

The Sister got a staff nurse to take him to a cubicle, set her to dressing the scratches. She had already bleeped Mr. Ellis, the Senior Registrar, and he arrived quickly.

"Your brother's for admission, but not to worry yet. He was in this accident and he's had a tap on the head. I think it will be twenty-four hours in for observation. With luck he'll go home tomorrow."

She went along the corridor and told him the story so far.

"Peter Cunningham was dead on arrival. You know, new junior student – fair-haired chap, father's a G.P."

They went to the side-cubicle where Ellis Minor lay, and assessed his case. He was very agitated, but they thought the Sister's verdict correct.

"Peter Cunningham's dead, isn't he, and Copper too?" the boy said. "They were riding in front and they took the full force of the wheel. Copper's in bits ... intensive care, but they'll not bring her back. She looked dead, same as Peter."

The Sister smiled at him.

"The alert call said you were all dead, but it was an

exaggeration. I'd stop worrying if I were you. A night in for observation and we'll probably discharge you all, and you'll get by with a headache. Most of your pals are minor theatre stuff – keep us busy all day. I'd not start worrying yet about Miss Rudd or anybody else."

The Nine-Pin Tragedy wound its way along. The police had cleared the scene of the accident and the traffic was rolling again. The police had had the lorry towed out of the meadow and held it for investigation as to road-worthiness. There were people to give statements to the law and long typed reports to do.

Casualty was busy all day, and two extra anaesthetists had been brought it. Mostly it was fracture work and minor surgery. The ordered chaos of Casualty cleared very slowly. At intervals more patients arrived with nothing whatever to do with the accident. A boy had swallowed his sister's hair-clip. He went to X-ray, but before anything could be done, his mother found the clip in his pocket. It was as well to be sure. The X-ray was negative, and they went home laughing. The work went steadily on. There was a queue for the plaster-room and cases for admission and cases for discharge.

"Just lie on the stretcher for a while and give it time to set. We'll send you home by ambulance. No, not now. If you want signatures you'll have to wait till tomorrow. We're a bit pressed today."

They were very tired, the staff. By eight o'clock the maze was almost disentangled. It was bad luck that a young mother came in with a screaming baby. It had not stopped all day, and they lived in a caravan. The father muttered that if the kid didn't bloody shut up he'd go home to his

Mum. There was nothing to be found wrong, but the infant went on screaming. They had been to Hunstanton for the day yesterday, and they had given it cockles to eat, and some ice cream – couldn't hurt him none.

After a long time he stopped of his own accord and was sent home to report the next day, unless he was perfectly well – then not to worry.

At midnight another 'Dead on Arrival' was brought in – an old lady who had stepped out under a taxi, and no time for avoiding her, and another shocked driver.

It was midnight, and Ellis Major was still on duty. Sister Norris had been on all day, but at last she was for her relief.

"It's time somebody did something about the traffic accidents in the city."

Mr. Ellis smiled at her.

"Didn't you look at the *Evening News* tonight, Norris? They're planning to put our traffic on the silicon chip system. Perhaps they'll stop the carnage, but I dare say it will make it all faster and worse."

He walked beside the Sister on her way to the exit.

"Anything new about Copper Rudd?"

"The Great Man was in to see her again at tea-time, didn't think much of her chances. He's coming back again at midnight to decide if he'll open her skull. She's 'prepped' for it, but you know he won't rush into anything, and her limb fractures are clouding the issues. He knows she's got a cracked head, but he's not convinced there's compression. Her general condition is worse and she's still on the respirator. She's about on the brink, I'm afraid – good material for the transplant boys. They've been alerted."

Sister Norris had seen the relatives arrive. They had

behaved very well. Yes, they were willing for transplant of any organs the doctors thought might help. Yes, they had signed the forms, had asked if there was anything they could do to help.

The Sister went off to her bed, and Ellis Major visited his brother. The hospital was dim and quiet. The never-ending corridors were dusky tunnels, but that only intensified the whispering. The whispering flowed like a tide from corridor to corridor, from ward to ward, from mouth to mouth ... through departments, through wards, from bed to bed and out into the forecourt, to McAlpine's army, which was never done putting up new departments ... It was one with the night, this whispering, and it widened like a dropped stone ripples a pool.

"Copper Rudd, the Lifeboat Girl. She's as bad as she can be. The surgeon won't be hurried. She's mortal bad, but he 'ont rush in. Let her lay tranquil, till she recovers a bit, but her limbs is broken every way and she's on extension for plaster. She hasn't breathed yet, but it will take time. She's on the iron lung. He's waiting from one hour to the next. He's the best in the country, the Brain Man. He'll do what's right. They have her all ready now and all her hair shorn and her bandaged. She has tubes in her arm and up her nose, but she don't move. They can't get her to breathe spontaneously. That's bad. I reckon the whole hospital is waiting to see her take over her own breathing." "That's Copper Rudd, that was her on Telly a few years back. She swum through a wild sea off the East Coast and near lost her own life, rather than see her two dogs drown ..."

"Dare say she knows her boy's dead. Maybe she doesn't want to come back to live without him. Fine young chap he was and all his life before him. Then he was gone in the twinkling of an eye – only son too, and doing well at Wentbridge."

The names of Adam, Seth and Joshua Rudd began to appear in the Press and the old history was told again. The story of the Lifeboat Girl was revived in full force, and it went on from one day to another. There was no change in the consciousness of the patient. She varied little. Then one day came the headlines.

DAILY EXPRESS.
LIFEBOAT GIRL BREATHES SPONTANEOUSLY.
Copper Rudd is encased in plaster from hip to toe on both legs. Her head is in bandages. She is out of the respirator now, but has made no sign of consciousness. A marathon effort is being made to keep this girl alive ...

Pick up the *Wentbridge News* one day and read the bulletin on 'the University Student'.

At Wentbridge Hospital, our reporter got the latest news on Copper Rudd today. She is 'doing as well as can be expected'. This girl is putting up the fight of all time against death. Her parents visit her frequently, but the person, who has drawn everybody's attention, is her grandmother. Mrs. Margaret Rudd of Flint Cottage, Marram, which is Copper's home in Norfolk.

Margaret Rudd is the old lady who lost her husband and her two sons in the Lifeboat Service. She now sits by Copper's bedside, and she knows it might help if she talks to her granddaughter. She is deep Norfolk, and she talks to try to call her back to life in the voice that Copper has known and loved since she was a baby.

100

So day followed day, and weeks ran into months. The next year came and it went on in the same old way. It was rafty old weather in Marram, and the girl from the newspaper shop was glad to stop at the fire on her way out, after she had set the paper on the bar of the Lobster Pot Inn.

"Good news tonight, Mr. Marshall," she said, and the landlord opened the folded paper and gave a great hurrah, that startled his guests from their darts and dominoes and skittles.

They gathered round to see the headlines.

COPPER RUDD RECOVERS CONSCIOUSNESS.
SPEAKS FOR THE FIRST TIME AFTER MONTHS OF SILENCE.
"TIME WE GO HOME TO MARRAM, GRAN," SHE SAYS.

There was a great sense of thanksgiving with Len calling for drinks on the house. It was like a horkey. Billy Grimes stood over by the skittle-board and set his tankard down carefully on a table. He thought back to the time he had met Copper as she got off the bus on her first holiday from Hale's.

"Don't know yah! 'pon my soul! Don't know yah!"

He could see her now, tilting the hat with the blue and white ribbons over her nose.

"If I were to tell you how much I've missed you all ..."

Cor! They'd all miss Copper if ... Billy bought a Mars bar for the newspaper kid, and there couldn't be anything better than Mars bars the way her eyes lit up. They had all

101

gathered round the bar, and Jimma Grimes was running his finger under the printed head-lines.

Billy gave the skittle-ball an extra shine for luck and swung it in its orbit through the standing pins. There was a click and the pins should have been rolling, but they staggered and stood.

There was a solitary pin down, but eight standing proud. His mind went back to the Nine-Pin Tragedy, and he remembered how they said at first that every one of the nine students were killed by the old lorry wheel, but it weren't so. Jimma Grimes had said that Jehovah had changed his mind at the last moment.

'Why should I shoot for nine and only lay one,' Billy thought. 'Reckon tha's a 'omen. Our Copper will soon be tearin' up the harbour in the speedy boat.'

5

LIMBO-LAND

Bear with me. Turn back the pages of time, for muddled was time. I beg your forbearance. There are passages in this story which I could never have set down of my own knowledge. Maybe I darned in parts of what happened, from accounts people gave me, or from what I read in the papers, when the news was old. There were conversations with relatives and friends, snatches from somebody else's knowledge, somebody who had stood and watched what came about.

Give me leave to draw it all up into a cobbled patchwork of a story. It's the best I can do.

Just now, turn back time and be gentle with me. I want to go back to the time we planned an end-of-term party at Wentbridge University. I thought it a great idea to wear Edwardian gear. The search we had for a pattern for leg-o'-mutton sleeves! Mrs. Willson found it in the attic in her grandmother's trunk.

Somebody said the ladies were as pretty as a bunch of Unwin's sweet peas. Each boy had a white carnation. Maybe I dreamt that there had been a Ball at King's and breakfast on the river. I could only think of the great wheel that came bowling at us out of nowhere. Smash! Crack! Tinkle! Tinkle!

There was nothing after that. I slept a strange sleep, but there were people speaking off-stage. I had no wish to be wakened.

There were strangers that lived at the other side of the wall, and they wanted to get in. There were lights that flicked on and off, and maybe mechanised things that ticked or rang, or bleeped or crashed metal against metal. I did not know where I was or what I was doing. I had to lie still and wait. I had no option, for I was bound hand and foot. I must lie still and wait. There was pain most of the time, but if I could forget it, it went away and I slept. I must lie still and wait ... still and wait ... still and wait.

"Just a prick in your arm, soon feel better, but I don't think you know us yet."

"Just a tiny needle again. It's not much."

They were all different voices. Over and over and over again, and so it went on, and after a lifetime the bright voices went out.

"It's been four weeks, you know," somebody said, but I was away in another world, out beyond the stars. At least this room had a window. Then I saw it was no window, only a place they put X-ray plates and turned them on and off, slotted the pictures into them and muttered with their heads together. I had no sense of time, for now there was a window, and when I looked out I saw sun and white clouds, and I was very high up. I was half-way up the sky and I was near the coast, for the sound of the sea was in my ears and I could hear the voices of some people I knew in the cottage, and I did not know what cottage. Maybe the sea was at gale force. I listened for the maroons to sound, but I could not think what maroons were. Mother was crying and Father would be sure to have his arm round her. Gran was put out about it, because they were trying to make her go home. How could she go home? We must all be at home, and yet this was not the place I lived.

"I'm set here and here I stay, till there ain't no cause for staying. Come you in here time you can. I'll be set here mardling still. There's times when I nearly reach her and then she's away agen. I'n't it a pity ya'd not tell her what's gone on at home? Ya're wasting your journey if ya' just sit whittling. She's be wanting to hear about little ole Skippy. Surely he'll be set on a walk down to the harbour. He'll be wanting to see the flood tide today and see how far the water's riz."

People disappeared and were back again, and it could be dark or dim or nothing. There were white starched flying butterflies. Sometimes I saw masked faces of chalky ghosts with only the eyes alive. They came and looked at a person in the shadow of the end of the bed. She was very ill. She was encased in plaster of Paris. Gran said that nobody need be frightened. The girl's hair had grown again, and it was mighty pretty. She took the girl's right hand and guided it up till the fingers touched the curly hair, but the girl did not comprehend.

"Hair's always curlier if it has to be shore off. There was no choice, and we knew it would grow again. Think how handy it is when you goo for a swim – shake your copper top and it will curl bright in the sun agen."

She changed her conversation with that strange sudden way she had.

"Would ya' not like to take ole Skippy along to the Martello Tower ... see Mistress Rouge again? She must be pining for ya!"

There was a picture of Robert Penn on the wall. Then I saw it was only an X-ray frame. He had silver hair, I knew, but they switched out the X-ray and the man was gone.

"She's not any better, is she, Mrs. Rudd? We have to face up to it."

I remembered Gran's 'backs to the wall' voice.

"She ain't any wusser, Commander. Remember that hymn she has such a shine for, 'Eternal Father, strong to save!' I know she's low tonight, but she's a 'Marram Mussel'. Is it high tide on the coast?"

"It's a flood tide."

"They go out with the tide along Norfick shores. She'll last out the darkness and then I have a feeling that she'll think it's time to turn for home. Don't break your heart over her, Commander. She'll look over her shoulder tonight and then she'll get better."

I knew Robert Penn from somewhere, but I could not place him. His hair was silver, but it was a family characteristic. He went off through the door, and I tried to run to follow him and my legs would not move. There was a Sister at a desk writing, and she came over to look down at me.

"Your plasters must be changed tomorrow. Let's hope was see some progress this time."

She smiled at Gran and told her she was working too hard.

"You've not been away from that bed for twenty-four hours every day, Gran."

"When Copper's better, then I'll rest, but I've got a rare feeling this last few days. It's time she began to make a fight for it. I said to myself, maybe it's now ..."

Who was Copper? I wondered. Why were her legs so slow to mend? Then there was a switch in time, and another ward that faced the country fields. The left leg was bare of plaster – bare, under a cradle, of any dressing whatever. There was an ugly puckered scar down the thigh. I was glad the other leg was still in plaster. Now the girls had come to move my arms again and press my ribs. Soon all my dressings would be off and I'd feel better.

The plaster cutters bit my knee and the blood ran redly, and 'Sister Orthopod, B five' was furious. I had no idea what was going on, but it seemed no matter. There was a little nurse crying. I focused my attention on the glass table and saw it had wheels. There might be a key on it, for I felt like Alice in Wonderland. If I could get the key and open the door, but I was flat on a white bed, that thrummed under me from a plug in the wall. Ripple, ripple, ripple ...

"Far rather have my goose-feather bed in Flint Cottage," said an old lady who sat at my side. "I usester lie in that bed and know Adam would come back to my arms, cold from the rafty weather, but there was a night when he never came, nor Seth nor yet Joshua – only young Noah left ..."

I tried to reach for the glass key, but it was gone. There was a pack of cards that played croquet on a college lawn. It was a long time ago, but there was snow feathering the sky and I was puzzled how it could snow in summer.

"That a little bit better, isn't it?" one of the people they called 'staff' said. "There's the best result of plastic surgery I ever saw out of India. It's a hair-line scar, can't even see what was all puckered gobbledegook.''

Then Gran's voice took over the conversation, and she and I were alone, and both my legs were under a rest and no dressings. If I did not look as if I were dead, I thought, they were fine.

"They'll be visiting today. Will I ask them to bring in the Penny Box for you from the chimney-piece?''

The girl remembered nothing.

"Marram, they'll be leaving Marram at noon,'' Gran said. "I hope they make it through the snow.''

I noticed she was very warmly dressed in a fine old navy reefer over-coat with brass buttons and a head-scarf round her ears. She was going away somewhere and perhaps she thought I would miss her.

"Sister Rose is taking me fer a walk to the colleges, see the aconites.''

It was morning, but not that day, for Gran was in her best black dress with the lace collar. She was sitting on her customary chair, smoothing out the white apron, and she had taken the girl's hand in hers, had leaned over, very serious sounding. I wished the girl would listen to her.

"Tha's February, lass. Time you wuz awake. The snow lays in patches still and you've been a powerful time asleep. Sister Rose took me to see they aconites by the river last week. They wuz a great sheet of gold. Time you saw 'em agen – must ha' seen 'em each year. That ain't so cold with the little brave flowers. You'll see the daffydowndillies soon ...''

There were shadows that lived in my world, for Peter Cunningham was dead. His parents had come to visit me a long while ago, and his mother's tears had wet my face. It was in my past dreams. I remembered a nurse that used a square of gauze to dry my face, and how they had hurried Peter's mother away, how Peter's father had kissed my cheek as if he tried to dry the tears ...

"Daffydowndillies," Gran said again, and I opened my eyes, put up my fingers to feel the lashes moving, to see it was really Gran and me. There was understanding that flooded in with the sun, and maybe somebody had switched on the light over the bed. Gran held my gaze in the net of her eyes and sat very quietly, as if she was afraid of frightening something away.

"And in no time at all the bees will be out in the heath at Narborough, buzzing the spring ..." she whispered.

I took in a deep breath and let it out in a sigh that seemed to go on for ever.

"Reckon it's time I went home to Marram," I said. "You've sat by me all the night, haven't you?"

I turned my cheek against the pillow and felt sleepy. If I closed my eyes I would just drift away, but Gran had no intention of permitting that. She looked at me fiercely over the old Mazzawattee Tea Lady's glasses.

"I've set by you all the autumn and the winter and now the spring, Little Fish, but it weren't a high-qualified job like they nusses had to do. They was angels of mercy and they worked till they wuz nigh dead on their poor feet, fur the things they must brave – and only children, most of 'em."

She stood up and went to look out through the window.

"It were a long night and darkish a time or two. If only it pleased the Almighty to let you remember what went before ... when it happened. If only He can stretch out a hand and make you whole again."

I remember it in wisps and patches – not all as it was

maybe. There was a pale girl here most of the time, very ill, but you were there too. Just now, before I woke up, I distinctly recalled the day Robert Penn took you into the dentist's in Norwich and bought you what you called a 'pair of false teeth'. We all laughed about it, and I woke up laughing. I thought it was all ending, and if you hadn't been by my bed it would have ended, but it's the beginning. If I can go home to Marram it will all come the same. There's a place called Sea Lane. I've just to run down Sea Lane and along to the harbour well. There's a place you can plunge into twelve feet of green clear water at high tide – water that wouldn't fail to wash the mist and the cobwebs away … Maybe I said it. Maybe I only thought it. I heard nothing.

Her face flinched against the pain she felt, for she had turned back from the window and I could see her clearly. Her hand reached behind her, and Gran had never been one to hide from the merciful quick blow.

"No lies now, Miss, no pretences."

She was always saying that in the old days to my child self.

Now I saw that she had picked up two elbow-crutches. I knew I would not, could not, walk without them. There was no chance of running down Sea Lane, Marram. To myself I admitted that I might never run again – walk even again. At the same time, I had Flint Cottage in every detail. In my mouth was the taste of the sticky buns, and Gran was back to sit in the arm-chair by the bed, setting the crutches by my hand, her voice a whisper.

"There's a way to goo yet and I'll bide till you're fit, do it take ever so long. You get your wits awake proper and walking 'ill not best you. All the same, there's a long haul yet …"

She pressed the bell that hung by my hand, and I supposed she thought it past time to call a nurse. The sound of the bell down the corridor reminded me of bicycles and leg-o'-mutton sleeves in Edwardian dresses one Midsummer's night and perhaps I had gone full circle, but it had not been like that. I had lain in the bottom of a deep dark pool and the light came seldom. It came dimly and with no sense in most of it, and I have put it down here the best I can.

I knew that the nurse that came in was a real person, for all that she looked like a Dutch doll, with her eyes a-blink in surprise. I felt a hand on my pulse and a thermometer popped into my mouth. The girl in the bed was myself. My copper hair was shorter. The nurse was at a loss what to say to me, so she said I was much better, wasn't I? and grinned at Gran. Then Sister Rose was there, and that was the first time I saw her for certain. She put her hand over mine.

"You've kept us all very busy. We'll have to take it easy now for a bit, but for all the surgeons may say, I think that if we get you to the sea and throw you in deep enough, you'll swim."

It was so strange to hear her laughing, that perhaps I went asleep again. I heard her tell Gran that there was no worry. This was a natural sleep and would do me good. So the long haul started.

One moment I would be clear enough in my mind and the next would come the dream state. I might have looked in a mirror at my reflection and then blown my warm breath to make a mist. It was like nothing as much as the

111

way the heavy coastal mists drift in.

Here was the man I thought of as the 'head doctor'. I did not quite know if he was 'a doctor of heads' or 'the head of all the doctors'. I was on a stretcher and they were taking me down to the clinic.

"It's nice to have you with us again. We're going to take another reading of your brain. You may remember it from last time? You're not frightened are you?"

I shook my head.

"It's no worse than a perm," said somebody called a 'Technician', but I did not think it necessary to tell her that I hadn't to have perms. I was feeling drowsy, so I closed my eyes, and when I opened them again I saw that they had moved me nearer the doctor's desk.

"There are some questions I want to ask you," he said. "First of all, can you tell me the date?"

I had no idea what date it was. It was extraordinary, but the time of the year had lost all interest to me. I looked at him blankly and said, "Only the aconites."

There seemed no continuity in the conversation.

"What monarch reigns England now?" he asked.

Then a moment after, when I still did not answer, he asked me the names of the Royal children.

"Royal children?" I repeated like any parrot, and I was afraid now. There was a throbbing pain in my temples.

"Post-concussional confusion," he said. "Besides, we had to look inside there. These things take time. Just have patience. You have excellent personality, and that's everything in these matters. Let's review the whole situation in three months' time."

"Three months!" I said. "Do you think I'll ever walk again?"

"That's not my field," he smiled. "I've given my opinion that you'll never be up to reading medicine. It's brought you top damages in court, which will be some consolation. We'll have to leave your walking powers to the Orthopaedic Department, and they're full of hope. The plastic surgeons have given you back your beauty, and really you're a credit to the art of medicine and surgery. You must remember all the road accidents in this University city which do not end so happily as you've done."

"As I am, what use am I? I'll be a burden."

"And that's depression, Copper," he said. "It's to be recognised and conquered. I know your family history. I know of the Rudds, who never gave up on any try. If you were to die, you'd have done it out on that village road with your dead boy's hand in yours. No trouble to anybody. As it is, you'll sit it out and you'll win. See if I'm not right. Meet me in five years and find yourself cured – find yourself almost back to what you were. Trust me, Copper. I know."

He came past my room to speak to me a few days later and met me struggling along the corridor, a nurse each side of me and the elbow-crutches clanking like assault rifles.

"Copper, my friend! Don't be impatient. Hasten slowly! You'll walk the sands and fish the seas again. You're going to build such a new life for yourself, every bit as happy as the one that fate knocked out of your hand."

He took the place of one of the nurses and walked me back to my room, dismissed everybody, but himself and me.

"I hope you remember that the university career is out. I did tell you. It's time we put it to you openly and see that you comprehend it. The damages have been assessed generously. The other side admit liability. The lorry 'was

113

proven' to be faulty. I like that Scots word 'proven'."

He went after a while, but he was back again in a week, and it was in his room and Gran was there and my parents and Commander Penn, and all of them mighty serious.

"Dr. Cunningham had been awarded a record sum of money," my father said. "What good does it do him? He 'oont beget the pride of a son again."

"I agree that money is nothing," the surgeon said. "It would be impossible to compensate the girl for what she's lost and suffered. Maybe she'll walk on iron sticks, but I think she'll walk naturally after a while. She has these 'petit mal' spells. She calls them her 'sea fogs'. She has a loss of sharpness of thought. She had mislaid the rapier of her wits, but she'll find that again. A brain can mend one hundred per cent. Do you hear that, Copper?"

He gathered us all up in one glance.

"*She* must never and *we* must never forget that she was once a girl who swam a few acres of angry sea, with two dogs by the scruff of their necks – and made it. Her grandfather gave his life and her two uncles did – she's got a Gran like granite. She's got to make another swim ... against another treacherous sea ... of bones that won't knit and flesh that won't heal, but it is healing already. There's no reason, as the Chinese would say, for bad thoughts. It will all come about if we give it time. I promise you. Besides, Copper, Commander Penn confided in me that he finds your vagueness attractive. No man wants a high-powered professional woman, Penn says. 'Buttons and bows,' he said, 'a lady of imagination and dreams'. He said it out before us all. The guardianship is to continue, too, and she must write the letters as she did formerly. I can't see why we are not certain of the victory."

He smiled over at me and knew that I did not comprehend it all.

"It's all in your head. You can do it," he said. "No bad thoughts."

I think Robert Penn drove my parents home to Marram, but I was in Ellis Major's room and he was having a talk with me. I knew him as the big brother of Ellis Minor, who had been at the Midsummer party that night, and he was grinning.

"You'll have to work hard at hydrotherapy, Copper. Our plastic surgeons have done miracles. Look at that suture. You won't remember where it was summer after this. Your legs are perfection, but we want some movement in them. For Pete's sake, look at your plates. Your fractures were comminuted – that means in bits."

I could remember nothing of the summer, autumn and spring. I did not want to look at smashed bones. It was summer again, and Ellis Major was full of 'the case of Thulbourne Contractors versus the Nine-Pins.'

"You weren't called to appear in court," he said. "The medical evidence clinched it. I know money means nothing, but those Contractors paid out handsomely. Did you see the headlines. *HALF A MILLION POUNDS FOR NINE-PINS.* That's what it said. It was plastered across the *Wentbridge Evening Press* last night and a photograph of you all on the old bicycles."

'Maybe all our tears will not wash out one word of it,' I thought.

My Alice in Wonderland world was familiar now. I might find myself alone with Mr. Tulliver, the lawyer, and he would go on with Ellis's conversation.

"You will be a very wealthy young lady, Miss Rudd, and your guardian has kept in touch with us constantly. You recall him?"

I tried to concentrate.

"He sent me to Hale's and we became friends in a strange sort of way," I said. "He was lonely and he wrote through your office or through a club. He had a typewriter that blurred the 'u' into 'o's. Rudd came out Rodd. I could have recognised his typewriter, if ever I saw it. The 'U' was lower in the line of type too. It was like a thing you'd have in a detective novel ..."

I knew Robert Penn wrote detective novels in his Martello Tower, knew he wrote ship stories mostly, but also detective action. He had friends in the police and in Scotland Yard, and he said they 'gave him nuts and bolts'. He had been a good friend to me for the last year, but Mr. Tulliver was keen to arrange for me to write to my guardian as soon as possible. It fitted in well enough with Cloud Cuckoo Land.

"I called my guardian the Penny Box Man. I don't know if he liked that."

"He liked it very much indeed," Mr. Tulliver said.

It became more and more difficult to remember Peter Cunningham. People moved like chess pieces through my life. Most powerful were Gran and Robert Penn. The Commander seemed to have taken on a new dimension of reality – and authority over what I did or did not do. He took over more and more of my hospital existence. He drove to Wentbridge from Marram every second day, and sometimes he brought the dogs with him. He harried my

116

attendances on all the departments – physio, orthropod, medical, surgical, brain.

I could walk now, but I must still use the crutches – only for another few weeks. Then I might run. I thought I could run and I tried it secretly and fell and kept a still tongue. They gave me an electrically propelled wheel-chair, and I took to haunting the corridors, sick for speed.

"I'm not dangerous," I'd laugh at some frightened patient and sent the fear from her face. This was an awful place. I had hoped to spend years here as a doctor, but that was a thought to be put out of my head. I was getting better now rapidly. My muscles were almost as good as new. I was getting confidence. I knew I could make it. My mind was sharp enough to get by. The fog drifts came seldom. My sutures were good. My bones were united, foolproof, or practically so. There was little fault to find in me. Only I knew the skin-grafts and the steel plates. I knew myself a dusty patchwork doll that life might leave in the gutter. I was as sick for home as ever Ruth had been amid the alien corn.

It was a great joy to have Mary Canning a resident student in the Complex. She was attached to the team, where Ellis Major worked, and I knew she was in love with him. They spent a great deal of time and attention on me, and the months slid by. Then at last I was almost due for discharge home. Mary gave a party in her room, and I shared their happiness – knew to the bottom of my soul, with a terrible poignancy, how it might have been for me if the circumstances had worked out differently. I pictured how it would be for them, working here together perhaps or maybe in a country practice … family practice and maybe the same families for forty years to come ... getting old, seeing their own children about them ... the practice children and the grandchildren too.

Peter Cunningham was dead. The others had all gone their ways and, perforce, they had left me behind. I felt as lost as I had done that first evening in Hale's Chapel. It was time to take myself off to bed. I slipped quietly away and tucked Gran into her bed with a glass of warm milk and a tablespoonful of 'ward' whisky. Then I remembered the letter to my guardian still unwritten, and tomorrow I would be away. I got out my writing-paper and sat up against piled pillows in bed and thought – at last made a tentative start.

Dear Penny Box Man – I left him behind at Marram and I asked your permission to change Mr. Nemo Blank – or did I?

I've almost left it too late, for the day after tomorrow, they promise me, I go home. I sit here and can think of nothing to say to you. It has had no reality to it. I think I used to tell you my innermost thoughts, so I'll do just that again, or try to.

Tonight I had supper in Mary Canning's room, and Ellis Major was there. You will remember Ellis Minor, his brother, in Hale's. He was one of the ill-fated Nine-Pins. Both Ellis boys are doing well. Peter, my Peter, is dead. I can't reach him any more. I cannot even convince myself that I loved him truly once. The others had all moved away from me up along the terms, and they are busy about their own lives. Mary has kept in touch, and I can never repay her for what help she gives me. I know myself ungrateful for feeling that I am like one of these great spacecraft, these new missiles aimed at a distant planet. I hit target and that was the end of my expected planned life. Thereafter I branched off out into uncharted space and so will continue on and on and on for ever.

Forgive me my grimness. I would like to tear this letter up and start afresh. Instead, I will tell you of the Christmas Swimming-Gala in the Complex Baths. The baths is like a stadium, international standard, and I am invited to a reserved seat for tomorrow night. I am not to take part, Marram Mussel that I am, but I may watch only.

The porter at the traffic barrier is a super swimmer, even though he dates back to the Second World War. He is to be the comic, diving off the high board in a red striped costume – and all his tricks go wrong, which is more difficult than if they went right. Kitty from Casualty, a very overweight orderly, is his assistant, and it's mostly her fault that he goes wrong, and it's all killingly funny. There will not be a seat empty, and, of course, Father Christmas will end up fully clothed in the water and have to be rescued.

There will be a beauty parade of some kind or another, probably from the typists' pool, and the secretaries will end in the pool, too, if they don't walk carefully. They have to use a cat-walk, which just asks for accidents.

So we will have all those atrocious examples of medical humour and everybody will laugh themselves sick.

They were kind to ask me. Gran won't go. I'll be with the Sisters, and that's high honour – and safe.

I know I ought to feel grateful, but I want to go home and not wait for this. The rules must be obeyed, no matter how foolish. I must be seen by 'the doctor' before I am discharged. He comes back from leave tomorrow, and no knowing what time he may arrive. I must wait till the day after. At least I can thank him. I must thank you, too. For a time I forgot all about you, and now I recall you with joy. When I woke up, after a time, you were there. I shall never think of you without gratitude, but suddenly I'm sleepy, discontented, too, to

119

*realise what I have become. I'm better, but it was nothing I did. I lay
like a smashed doll, and life came about me again instead of going
away – would not go away. The ants worked ceaselessly. I slept
maybe for ever.*

*Goodnight, my familiar friend, my kind-faced, caring Penny Box
Man. I will go and post this now. It is strange to think that your
hand will open the seal. I must address the envelope as always to Mr.
Tulliver at Lincoln's Inn Fields, and he will send it to you by return,
as he always did. This I remember clearly enough – all I must do is
to lick the stamp and fix it in the top right-hand corner ...*

I got the sudden idea of doing something forbidden as
any sin I had ever contemplated. I knew that the
swimming-bath was closed and dark and silent, all ready
for the Gala the next night. I had only to put on the white
swim-suit I used for Hydrotherapy, and the scarlet
towelling-wrap that reached my finger-tips. A dressing-
gown was good hospital disguise. I was wearing sandals. I
went down the back way after a quick check that Gran was
fast asleep, snoring a little in her nose. Here was the post
box and my guardian's letter on its way, and here was the
outer door and darkness after the bright of the top hall.
After a long time I saw that the windows of the baths were
black, thanked God that the door was not locked. Inside,
the water glittered in the moonlight through the glass roof,
and I was afraid. They would not let me swim tomorrow.
They might never let me swim again. There was trouble
with one of the plates, but there was often trouble with
plates – not to worry.

On the walk to the edge I discarded dressing-gown,
towelling-wrap, one sandal and then another. I stood on the

edge with my toes gripping the tiles, and then turned back and limped on my crutches to the switches. I pressed one and then another and prayed nobody noticed from outside. I went back to the edge again and looked up at Carnival. Christmas Present was here and now. There was holly and ivy and mistletoe, and a scarlet tower for some Romeo and Juliet act. Here was a corral of pumped-up rubber horses with funny faces, a pile of life-belts, some rubber dinghies, grotesque masks on the white pillars, white tickets reserving seats ...

One, two, my crutches clattered on the tiles and I held my breath, against listeners at the door. I stood as still as any statue, knowing I would never swim any more. Oh, but it was good to stand so on the edge of a dive, even though my heart was breaking. I was 'the Little Fish' – or was I? The Marram Mussel?

I heard the door open behind me, slamming back loudly, and knew I was discovered. I judged it was my last chance at life – knew it as the truth. At my feet I saw again the white horses of the wild seas that day at Marram, saw again Rouge's tawny fur roll under the surface, saw the splash as old Skippy's cobby body hit the tide. It did not matter that Skippy was dead and gone and another Skippy had reigned in his place and another. Our Jack Russells, our dogs, our faithful Skippies – Gran never called a dog 'ought else'. Their spirits came back and inherited the little bodies "Kinda soul cages," Gran said. They came looking for us – and all the same old tricks.

My body took the surface and left it nigh unbroken, and I was into a smooth fast crawl, but with a strange glory about it, the same as it had always been – my element. The tiles at the far end found my reaching fingers, and I was round and under and a push of my feet to send me away, and now it was the underwater run, full length of the baths and the gift of the ability to do it, and the feeling as if my heart would burst with gratitude for resurrection. Then the tiled wall again, and my head breaking water, and two chestnut polished shoe-caps that stood waiting.

Robert Penn had arrived at the Complex and seen the lights and guessed what I had done. There had developed this extra-sensory perception between us long ago. He had known I must prove myself. He had interpreted the cause of the lights in the windows. He had come running. I reached for the edge to hoist myself up, but his hands had mine and I was lifted level with him, the towelling round me, my hair tousled.

"Well done! You had to do it sometime. This was as good a time as any. Now you know! You're the same girl that swam the seas that day after the dogs – always will be. Nothing can change that, nor ever will."

I pulled on my dressing-gown and pushed my feet into my sandals – walked off to the door without my crutches, but he carried them after me.

"It's as well to use them till we get you back to your ward. One of these days we'll lay them aside, but not yet. Your swim-suit will dry overnight, if you put it on the radiator. Let it remain a secret between us, that you're still the 'Little Fish' ..."

He stooped and kissed my cheek and was gone, as if he had never been. The night night the Gala was superb. Then the day after it was time to go, and Robert took us to Marram – Gran, dogs, luggage and all. He was given to opulent vintage cars, and first of all he had had the Daimler, but it was long gone. This year he had achieved a Rolls-Royce Coupé – a long chocolate car with a gold stripe on the body-work – that would turn any head in any street in the world. These opulent cars were a thing with him, and I never knew whether he told the truth about their value. For all I knew he might be very rich, but I rather thought he was not. "Money doesn't matter," he always said. "Happiness counts." Gran was very proud of riding in a Rolls, for she maintained that a hearse might be her only chance at that, and we all laughed a lot. Skippy was hysterical with delight and barked non-stop in towns. Robert had recently replaced Rouge by a male puppy and was still mourning old Rouge.

"Damned if I don't call him Rouge too. He'll catch her soul and stop chewing the carpets. Isn't that right, Gran?"

It was a lovely evening as we ran across Narborough Heath and over the rise and down the long slope to the sea. It was twilight before we came in sight of the North Sea, and my heart was thumping my chest as the road drew near Sea Lane.

Maybe Billy Grimes had been waiting 'a-purpose' in his butcher's straw hat, on his old bicycle, Grimes and Son, a foot on the ground to steady him and his round face breaking onto a melon-seed grin at the sight of us.

The delicate purr of the Rolls may have been ousted by his loud 'Hullo', but my heart was lifted to heaven. I had come home. " 'Pon my soul, don't know yah!' "

He rode quickly up the lane in front of us, and Robert had perforce to slow down. Then 'Trabb's Boy' spun down a path and appeared right in front of Flint Cottage, pulled

123

up short beside us and surveyed the whole equipage.

" 'Pon my soul," he said, "you're so proud grow'd!"

That was how I came home to Flint Cottage, and I recognised it as the place it had always been and would remain to be. Marram had not changed in any particular whatever, only that mists rolled in from the shore sometimes, when only my eyes saw them. It was no great important matter, but it was strange the way maybe it was Billy Grimes who saw to it, that I understood it that day.

6

INTERVAL FOR TWO VILLAINS ...

With hind-sight I should think that the strange interval went something like this. I have no way of knowing, nor will I ever know, for sure, but a deal of my history is like that ...

Take a grey grim building and a room in it, grey and grim too. It had rained all day, and it was as if the rain had penetrated the walls to bedew the paint. You could run your finger along the damp glass, that was chipped cream above and chipped green for wainscotting, leaving a snail's trail.

The window was too high to see anything but the leaden sky and the tears of the rain on the panes. There were two men, one at each side of the table, and they were well familiar with dank cheerlessness and the smell of institutions. They had just finished a game of crib, and the cards were thrown down. The elder of the two rolled himself a cigarette and lit it with a flick of his nail on a red-headed match. There was a copy of the *Eastern Daily* flung on the floor, and he picked it up, assembled the pages into some kind of order and studied the racing-news, yawning with the drag of time.

"Yarmouth was a washout," he said.

The younger man had collected the cards, as if to have another game, but he was bored too. He fanned the pack out and slid them back in formation again, as if he played an accordion. He dealt a suspect hand to himself, with four aces on top. He watched his companion spread the paper out on the other side of the table and thought that Bert had lost his boredom suddenly. He looked as a pointer might, scenting game. There was obviously something in the *Eastern Daily*, but Bert was going to keep him waiting. Besides, the man had no learning. He always read slowly, his head one side, squinting his right eye to the page and running a finger under each line of print.

It was a front-page article and there were two full columns. He went right to the end of it and then back to the top again and so to finish it at last, and still he said nothing. The pale young man grew impatient, but he kept his impatience to himself, only for gnawing at an already bitten-down thumb-nail.

"There's a winner in here for ya', Major – just up your street. Don't never say I can't spot form."

It was all being slowed to exasperate him, the dark man knew, knew that he was out of place in such company, wondered how he had ever got there in the first place, and said nothing.

"*Modus operandi*," said his companion, and he pronounced it wrongly as usual. "You won't have any great planning to do on this 'ere. It's like an advert put in for you and me."

"And we're available, or soon will be," said the dark man, and smiled away his ill-humour.

At that, the paper was spun about on the table and there lay the article for reading.

The Major took it up and sat back in his chair, and there was breeding in him.

"God! Do they ever wonder, when they send us to these places, that there are times when a chap would sell his soul for a bottle of whisky?"

Then the article trapped his attention, and he was skimming it, returning to read it as slowly and deliberately as the older man had done. The overhead light might have shone his black hair to patent leather, but his hair lacked its usual oiliness and was unkempt. His voice was pleasant. His smile lit his face with humour, and he was a presentable man with the hallmark of army training about him.

"My dear friend, it's tailor-made. You certainly have hit the gold at last. Everything is there – the time, the terrain. Near enough, I was a boy in this place, but they won't remember me. There's a pub on the coast near the village – a hostelry – out of the way ..."

He put the paper on the table and rested his elbows on the front page, his head in his hands.

"Let's think now. It's called some fish name – the Lobster Pot, if I'm not wrong? We'll play it like last time – the good old *modus operandi*. It was the Barley Mow last time, though we didn't bring the harvest home, but this looks good. It's taking sweets from a kid. They're honest simple people – no high-class know-how wanted."

"She's a rich little bugger all the same," grinned Bert. "It ain't fair when you think of it. They wasn't up to nothing, was they, them kids? They wasn't even smashing telephone kiosks nor that sort of vandalism. They wasn't breaking, nor yet entering. They was just having theirselves a good time."

The Major picked up the paper and leafed through it, muttered that there was no photograph.

"One has a certain regret," he said. "This poor girl is going to need help and support. She'll hardly be all that attractive with what they say went on. Still, we can't have everything, and if she's educationally subnormal, all the better – for us."

"They're fisher folks," Bert pointed out. "It'll be kidding the natives. She'll be as soft as skit, and they're honest simple people. We'll do it easy."

There was a mental picture going up, as if the dark man had a computer in his brain, flashing the whole complete set-up.

The Lobster Pot was right off the beaten track. They might have more fun in Yarmouth. He'd put Yarmouth as second choice. It would be better to snatch the car 'up in the smoke'. He was grateful for some plans to make. There was the 'recce', the kit and the cash. He looked at himself in the glass on the wall and knew that he had not lost the stamp of public school. Just let his hair grow a bit. It had been the O.T.C. It had given him the military look that had spawned the undoubted fascination he had for women.

"I'll want a chauffeur and batman."

"That's O.K., mate, be glad to sign on with 'the Don' again."

The Don's mind was away with the years. In school the boys had counted the days till the end of term, when they were 'out'. On the wall here was the calendar of crossed-off dates, below the nude dream-blonde. He turned over the months and gave the score softly.

"Three months and six days, unless ... unless ..."

"We ain't going over any wall. Good behaviour, that's our motto."

"It will be pleasant by the sea come April, May, June. We'll set it up and we won't be in a hurry this time."

He had never forgotten the old school. The stores-keeper here had three ties of the colours with his gear in the office. Maybe it proved something, but those ties were his 'stock in trade', and that was a laugh. The Chapel had fixed itself in his memory, and in a way he had loved it. It was the Chancel, where the sixth-form boys sat, each on high mahogany with a single candle burning in a globe before them, reflecting everything everywhere in the high shine. The mahogany was polished – by the years. It was unforgettable for ever. It was a pity he had not done better, but he'd made a fresh start now and the sea might turn the tide of his luck. There was a hymn, they used to sing in chapel, if a storm came up. It related the present to perfection. Bert might understand the joke. Bert had done a stretch at the North Sea Camp and called it 'Arctic hell' on the salt marshes. Bert sang 'like a hoarse mavish' after filling sandbags for the defences against the north-easter.

Back to the present. It was time for the light bulb to come on, but the dusk had taken over. One of the screws had gone off for a cup of char, most likely.

The Don knew that the North Sea could change its mud colour to the blue of the Med, come April, May, June. Then came the summer storms too. There was a grey clay tinge to his own face in the mirror, but he had the look of an Adonis, no, maybe an Achilles with a feathered-arrow aimed at his heel. He wanted somebody to look after him. There was a hunger for kindness about him, but nobody had cared for him, since the day he was born. It showed, and it made women vulnerable.

The girl lived with her people by the sea and her forefathers had gone down in ships to the great waters.

He was back in the school chapel and the wind was howling the heavens. In his vast imagination the organ had gone into William Whiting's hymn.

Eternal Father, strong to save ...

He smiled at Bert as he joined his memory in a voice that might have been Bing Crosby's baritone.

She lived on the coast did she?

Oh, hear us when we cry to Thee
For those in peril on the sea ...

There was a storm on its way.

7

FIRESTORM

Sometimes in the morning I woke up, wondering where I was, who I was. There was a long panic that I might have skidded the earth and time. My eyes sought the windows, and my brain skeetered round space. This was not the white cube of Hale's bedroom-study. It was not the free luxury of the Willson's two rooms at Wentbridge University, for there was no traffic thrumming by. I was no longer half-way up the Hospital Complex sky. Then the murmuring of the tide would bring back Marram's flooding peace. I had only to see the old brass telescope that commanded the North Sea. It commanded the North Pole Star and put the universe in position. Up the coast was the Martello Tower, and I could snuggle down in bed for another ten minutes and think of Robert Penn – wonder if he was my North Pole Star, for it seemed so. I was becoming increasingly involved with Robert Penn. I had had a few years of extraordinary adventure, and I was back home again. Gran and Robert had followed me and brought me back to harbour. It was the same place, but changed. The Penny Box Man was the constant factor, there on the mantelpiece, but there had been a great unhappiness, and it was over. I had put the misery behind me, and I lived the same life that I had always lived in the holidays, yet not the same. I was a rich woman for one thing. That did not seem to matter, except if I wanted to buy anything I had only to put out my hand and sign a cheque. I could go 'up Lunnon' and get myself fabulous clothes, but I got little value from doing it. I could buy presents, and this was a great joy, for the people who received the presents with such enthusiasm only wanted to see me better. Gran took to wearing a seal-skin coat to church, and gritted her teeth to parade her pride in public.

It was in Robert Penn I found change. He had been my brother, my constant companion – friend against all the world. Now there was an awkwardness between us. He had been difficult when I asked him to help me with financial matters. He had taken to being awkward when no awkwardness should have been. Maybe I saw what was wrong at last. The fortune I had achieved through damages had changed me. I was not Copper Rudd any more, but a rich woman in my own right. He might be thought to be a fortune-hunter. That was the way with all foolish men. Could they not understand that the money meant nothing but only security? I had lost the bright dream. It was best to put it all behind me, and in a way Robert did not change, but in a way he did. His eyes told me he was in love with me and maybe I loved him. No maybe about it. I did love him. I valued being with him beyond anything. When he was with me the light switched on. I took to haunting the Martello Tower with the slightest excuses. I shared the day when I put aside the crutches for ever. We had dinner in the Lobster Pot, and a great celebration and hilarity, when I had attempted to teach Len Marshall, 'mine host', how to cook lobster thermidor.

I helped in Flint Cottage the shop and the fishing as I had always done – and was happy. My dreams of being a high-up professional doctor had been put aside for me. I was happy to wait ...

Besides, the Penny Box Man was not only a china money-box on the mantelshelf. He was the guardian who had tried to take me on a flight up the stars. It was not his fault that fate had stepped in, and he still wrote to me and I to him in the same confidential letters.

I stretched out in bed and knew that something odd had happened, but in the first hours of morning it hid from me.

Only a day or two ago I had met somebody of importance and he eluded me in the manner of nowadays. I had forgotten who he was in a blanking-out of memory. I had learnt how to deal with it by now. One did nothing. One hung round a bit and back it came like a carousel. I had just to lie as quiet as a hare in its form and shut my eyes against the world.

It was something that Billy Grimes had told me. That started it. I had gone down Sea Lane to fetch steak and kidney for a pudding from Grimes', the Butcher's Shop. Gran was going to start the 'swimmers' and that was Norfolk for dumplings.

"Boil it four hours or more," Gran said. "Can't boil it too much – not steak and kidney – five hours if you wish."

Don't puzzle to think. It comes back itself – always does. What does it matter?

Ah, yes! Billy had told me that there were visitors at the Lobster Pot. He had been in there on Sunday night.

The Penny Box

Billy was the son in Grimes and Son, and his mother was Mrs. Grimes, like all the other Happy Families of Marram. He had had the desk behind mine at school, that first day, but now he had grown up and was a partner in Grimes and Son.

'Conningsby', that's his name, this chap from away. He's got a super car and a 'shofer' kind of body servant. He booked a room for hisself in the Lobster Pot and another for the 'shofer'. Then he took the small private bar as a sitting-room – private for hisself, posh – a fire and all, and nothing but the best. He has his meals in there.''

I could remember all that Billy had said. There had been an empty shop, and Billy was not one to miss the chance of a gossip.

Mister Conningsby was a big chap, very dark and with a touch of the military about him. He had come into the bar, while the valet cleared his supper away, had talked to the fishermen, no pride to him. Some way, they had got talking about lifeboats. He had known about Coxswain Bloggs of Cromer, and they had told him about the Marram boat.

I was bored with that boat, God forgive me, and I knew Billy was capable of talking for ever, given a start. Billy had tried to interest him in the Nine-Pin Tragedy, but Mr. Conningsby had not been interested. He was bored with road accidents, especially as he had just been driven down the Great North Road on his way from what Billy called 'the He-brides'. He owned an island there. He set himself down in the inglenook 'agen' the fire, but first he called a round, but 'he weren't much for talking', just watched the fire as if he were hungry for warmth.

"The driftwood were sparkin' away and it almost put

134

him asleep, and then 'the shofer' came to tell him his bunk were turned down. That's grandeur for ya"!

It was past time to get up. I was due to go to sea with Father after fish. We had to lay lobster-pots, and I hoped that he had the baiting done and the pots in the boat. Gran fussed about me when I was having breakfast, and told me to wrap up warm. It might be summer, but there was a North Easter and black cloud on the way in.

"Put on that white fleece jacket you bought up Lunnon. Tha's a treat on you, mitts to match, and all, and that Jack-mar scarf. You might meet Robert Penn."

I told her I would be obliged if she would stop trying to woo Robert Penn, but she just made to box my ears for me and told me to be on my way.

"It's cold. I'll put a match to the fire 'fore ya' come home. Mind how you goo then."

I walked down to the harbour and wondered if my sophisticated clothing could be interpreted as lure for Robert. I admitted that I was hoping that he might have the speed-boat out today. We might take her for a run to Blakeney Point.

The harbour was as usual, and no Robert, but instead a very opulent car, black, glistening from polishing, and a man in a peaked cap and leggings about to put money in a slitted wooden box that somebody had clumsily nailed to the mast of the flag-pole. He was squinting an eye down to read the notice CAR PARK and looking rather puzzled at the four other cars parked with a fine carelessness. There was a man in the back of the car, engrossed in the sea, taking me in, too, as I stopped at the head of the steps. His hair was as black as a crow's and his eyes were the deepest blue, I had ever seen. His eyelashes were so long that they cast a dark shadow on the white of his face. He looked as if he had been ill. He started to get out of the car almost at my side, and I could not ignore him. He glanced at me and away again, and I remembered that Norfolk folk are honest. I must not see him robbed. There had never been a car park here and please God never would be! Some of the children had been up to ingenious mischief. I called out to the chauffeur that it was not necessary to pay to park.

"Some of the children have taken to crime. It's the sort of things kids get up to. I'll see to it personally, but don't be conned."

It all happened so naturally. We were all laughing, and the dark man had turned to thank me. When he smiled, his whole face changed. I had never seen anything like him. He had been perfection before, but now he was lit up from within with warmth and humour and kindness. If ever I had imagined the Archangel Michael, this was he. His voice was Wentbridge maybe and a touch of Scots.

"I'm Donald Conningsby. You find me lost – fallen among thieves. You're my 'good Samaritan'."

I grinned at him and told him we had no thieves in Norfolk.

"It's a local rule and I'm glad to help. I'm Hillary Rudd, and this is my father – Coxswain of the Lifeboat. He wouldn't tolerate crime in Norfolk. We'll be glad to put a stop to it."

"Ah!" he said, and again, "Ah!"

He took me in from head to toe.

"We say the same in the Western Isles. We don't even lock our cars there."

136

My father was coming slowly up the steps with a hand out in welcome.

"I'm proud to meet Coxswain Rudd. I've heard about your extraordinary lifeboat. I've got a thing about lifeboats. It must be something to have a family like yours."

He clapped Father on the shoulder and grasped his hand, said he was honoured.

"The boat's called the *Adam, Seth and Joshua Rudd*, Major, sir," put in the chauffeur, with a voice as gruff as a grizzly bear. "I had heard all about it from the men in the Tap last night."

But Donald Conningsby dismissed him with a smile and reminded him that they were low on petrol, waved away the offer of the return of the parking fee. It was obvious that his man liked him.

"We're staying at the Lobster Pot, ran down from the Hebrides. I've been ill and I had nobody to look after me. My man insisted that I get away. I had some virus or another."

He shook his head and said they must be off if they were to catch a petrol-pump before lunch-time.

"I'm at the Lobster Pot, but I told you that. Mine Host is a character. He sees after us well. He was in the Home Guards and tried to shoot down a V 2."

This was a joke, for V 2's were harmless as long as they kept on flying. His laugh maybe swept me off my feet. His head went back, and his eyes had silver fish that swam in the irises.

"They were unmanned planes that flew overhead, Miss Rudd, and when the engines cut you got yourself flat on the ground – and Marshall tried to bag one like a grouse, but I

137

doubt you were born then and neither was I."

He might have known us all our lives, and he carried happiness with him and joy and fun. He was magic. He was marvellous. I thought probably he was a Scots laird, for that was the cut of his jib. He had on a Norfolk jacket, a shooting-suit for a Scots moor. There was maybe Gordonstoun behind him and some Scottish Regiment. I settled for the Argyll and Sutherland Highlanders, and even fitted the swing of the kilt and the lilt in his voice and the skirl of the bagpipes to him. I shall never know how he worked such a charm on me, but work it he did. I had fancied myself falling in love with Robert Penn, but this was a firestorm. In five minutes I understood what it was to leave Mother and Father and brother and sister – lose all interest in ordinary things and cleave unto one man, but I knew it was quite impossible that it happened to me. I shut my eyes to it. There was a stained-glass window in our church at Marram, near to the pew we sat. There was an armoured knight who knelt to a sword. From the age of four I had known him as the Archangel Michael. Maybe he was and maybe he was not, but he had been my baby love – and now here he was on Marram harbour wall and his chauffeur in polished leather leggings. The likeness was in the eyes, just that same deep, deep blue. I was glad I was wearing the white fleece jacket and the mitts to match, the rust sail-cloth slacks, that had a Fortnum's cut. When had I cared for such things? There was this black bar coming up the horizon, and soon it would rain cold rain, and it was time I was getting out my oilskins. I put my hand in his and perhaps he took some notice of me, but I thought not. I jumped down into the stern of the boat, when I would far have preferred to get into the car with him. He wished us good fishing, and the chauffeur opened the back door for him, but not before Skippy had defended the boat against him.

"Game wee beastie," called my Scots laird. "He'd be useful in the hunt kennels."

He was courteous enough to watch us cross the harbour. Then the car swept a circle and was away. It stopped at the garage of Mr. Grimes, who was Billy's uncle. I got out the glasses and spied on them. They had reached the garage before lunch-time and the chauffeur was overseeing the filling of the tank. Major Conningsby had left the car and was watching our boat go out. He might see the glint of the sun on my binoculars, so I put them down, as if they were red hot.

"Lucky we saw that chap," Father shouted in my ear. "If we pick up a few lobsters, Len wants them over the Lobster Pot, wants them for Major Conningsby's late dinner. Lobster cold with a crisp lettuce. Lobster hot and buggered about a bit. That ain't called the Lobster Pot for nought. I thought I'd take them over myself, if we've caught good 'uns. Len don't want rubbish."

"I'll take them in the van, Father, be glad to. Len is bound to make a mess of lobster thermidor if I don't watch him, always has done."

I was being devious, for I did not tell my father that a firestorm had overwhelmed me. The rain was whipping us, but I did not find it an inconvenience. I was helping with the lifting, and laying fresh bait.

I was watching for specially big lobsters. Presently we were ashore with a record catch, and I was down in the basement, preparing lobsters *against thermidor*. I had rung Len Marshall and the Major preferred his lobster hot.

"I'll do it Len. Don't fuss yourself. I used to be 'prenticed to Madame Prunier's in Paris."

It was a joke that lasted. I prepared the lobsters. They met their fate in the fish basement. I put the finishing touches in the Lobster Pot kitchen, and Major Conningsby could never have known the care and attention his dinner had received.

Then I was caught in the act of changing his dinner-table as to a freshly starched cloth and fish cutlery, and perforce the Major discovered the stratagem. After all, this was only a country pub. I was invited to be his guest. If I had been so gracious as to catch the lobsters and then cook them, I must share the feast. It became tremendous fun.

I will never forget that dinner till my dying day. I might have wished to be clad in a dinner-gown, but I was still in slacks and a white polo-neck sweater. My fleece-lined jacket was flung on the kitchen settle. I sat at one side of the table and was glad I had had the setting of it. Bert, the chauffeur, waited on us skilfully, but there was no formality between us. He took part in the conversation and so did Len Marshall, and it was all typical of Marram, completely friendly and no starch except in the cloth. Bert complained that the Major did not look after himself. He had been 'born an orphan'. By this, the batman meant that his mother had died at his birth and his father had been killed in the previous war. He had known no family. A Post Humus child, as Bert had it.

"I reckon I'm his family, Miss Rudd."

He was reprimanded for this, but Bert was obviously an

old friend with great privilege.

"He owns an island in the Western Isles, and he's a prince up there, but things ain't what they used to be. He's only happy there, but times has brung him down like a hunted stag. He'd die to bring his clan to making a living wage, but the government leeches him. He'd never complain, if you tortured him."

I called him Donald by this, and the valet was in trouble for giving away private gossiping facts.

"Get out and give them a hand with the washing-up. If I feel like giving confidences, I'll give them myself. The lady isn't interested in me or my business."

I sat in the 'private sitting-room', which was the little bar, over coffee and Kirsch, and together we worked our way down the Kirsch. People called him 'Donnie'. He'd like it if I did. My wisdom varied with the level of the Kirsch. He wheedled my story out of me, and I told him too much of it, but he was one of these people who cared for the happiness of everybody in the world.

"Seems we're two of a kind, Hillary. You're lucky to have had a loving family. I'm a loner, always have been. In an army family one's forefathers are beneath tomb-stones or on brass war memorials in some kirk. Latterly, I've had only old Bert to give a damn about me."

"And all your people on your island?"

"They scratch up their living in the peat and the fishing. I've been no laird to them. I've got some snaps. I'll show you one day, but Bert and I must soon be away home."

I reminded him that he wanted to see the lifeboat, and he seized on the idea with enthusiasm. In no time at all I had a firm date to meet him at the R.N.L.I. Station.

The time came when we met, and I was a bird plumaged to attract my mate. I knew it – knew that I didn't suit Marram. Gran said I ought to have more sense than to wear scarlet nap with red hair, and asked what I was doing out in my best Harrod's outfit, messing about with boats. I felt 'prima'. I had the white skirt and sandals with too-high heels, and a scarf with what they called a sea-motif 'up Lunnon'. I knew I was being too show-off knowledgeable by far. I was relieved that Robert Penn was not within earshot.

I explained about the starting-pin for the launch of the boat. It was fortunate I did not actually launch the boat, so caught up was I in my emotions. It was tornado. I had forgotten them all. I was explaining the launch, taking a pretend swing at the pin, when I found myself in his arms. It was as simple as that. I launched something I could not even comprehend. I was swept up on a wave twenty feet high, that lifted me and rolled me and tumbled me to dizziness. His arms were about me and his mouth over mine. I knew I was in paradise, and I knew it was for eternity, for he felt for me as I felt for him.

It did not matter if they were against me. I forgot them all. The world was well lost, if I had Donald Conningsby and he had me.

It was all sunshine and pink champagne and rose spectacles. He kept me in his arms as he carried me on the crest of that wave, perhaps it was no wave, but a flight on a space-rocket, with comets that soared past us trailing flames. He loved me since the moment he had seen me at the car park, that wasn't. My face had been filled with the conviction that right should prevail. Would I marry him soon ... say I would ... soon ... soon ... soon.

He must meet my people and I must meet his. We hardly knew each other.

"Of course, I love you too, but you don't know anything about me. We're not grand people. We have a shop and a bake-house and fishing."

He had no intention of a long engagement. He wanted me now, but he might give me a week or two. He'd go and meet my people this minute ...

He was very masterful, and he tried to sweep Flint Cottage off its situation on the heights of Sea Lane. He was full of the exuberance of finding I adored him, and maybe he took it all for granted. I do not understand why they took a dislike to him. Perhaps it was because I was an only child. He was charming to Gran and kissed her hand, but she was unimpressed. She had a touch of the Gestapo about her. I knew she was thinking he was 'foreign folk'.

"We'll have to meet your kin," she mumbled, and he asked what was all this stuff about kin.

"My batman has it that I was born an orphan. I was a post-humous child like David Copperfield. My mother died ..."

Gran had no sympathy.

Mother was upset, and the shop was busy. She kept running in and out, and she was far too emotional. Every time she came back from the shop her eyes were pinker and pinker. It seemed that my kin was plain Norfolk stubborn, so I went in on his side and took his hand in mine.

"Donald wants us to get married soon. I've almost promised."

"When you go to 'chutch' with a man, that'll be done

143

praaper," said Gran, "with the engagement in the *Eastern Press* and the presents and the invitations, and the 'flaahs' and the cake and the trousseau ready and all your bottom drawer and that ..."

"We'll see about it, Mrs. Rudd," Donnie laughed. "Have you forgotten what it is to be young and in love? I will have my way you know."

"Marry in haste, repent at leisure," she cackled at me like a witch, and he let go my hand and took hers, kissed it again and was gone.

Then the storm broke. Father tried to stop it developing into a force eight. He reasoned with me to remember that I was only just recovered from a serious illness.

"You know you ain't as good at thinking. It's near enough clear now, that sea mist of yours, but to rush into marriage is daft. You don't know him and he don't know you. Is he able to care for you and cherish you as you've been cherished here all your life?"

"He has no family. He told you. He's a laird and he owns an island. You've seen the car he runs. He's gentle and kind. I won't change my mind. I love him and I'll always love him."

"And what about Robert Penn?" Gran demanded. "You're his girl or were. What are you going to tell him?"

I stared at her in amazement, but the thought of Robert had not even entered my head. I had imagined I loved him, but not in this hurricane way. I knew they were right and I should wait a little while, but they kept on saying things and I was stubborn. Mother said that probably I was not good enough for such a nobleman, nor strong enough after my illness ever to be a bride. I was not showing much wisdom this minute.

What use is there to think back on it? Donnie met them again after church on Sunday and was charming to them, but Flint Cottage had turned into a stable of mules. I was not my old self. I was infatuated by this stranger. I might announce the engagement and wait till a year had gone by, at least till I had been for my next appointment at the hospital, which was not for nine months ...

Robert Penn called the next afternoon and met Donnie, who arrived soon after him. They had behaved like two civilised gentlemen in an atmosphere of family row that you could cut with a knife. I took Skippy for a walk the next day, to spy out the land, went to the Martello and found Robert writing. He was sad. He had drawn away from me. He agreed with the family. He was still and formal – subdued.

"You're not in a state of health to make a decision like this," he said. "What do you think I've been waiting for?"

Then he veered away from that quickly and asked me not to go against my family. "They're older than you and wiser. Besides, Mr. Tulliver will have to be consulted. There will be legal matters. He's your solicitor, or I think you told me about him. P'r'aps not."

"Donald wants me and I want him. I'm grown up and I'm not a puppet any longer."

I knew myself changed from the old loving Copper, over those few days. I was no finished product of Hale's and Wentbridge. I understood where all those dreams and yearnings had been leading me.

Robert was away to London for a few days – asked me to wait till he came back. It was important to wait till he came back. I just shook my head and knew if I did not run away now I was lost. First I ran all the way to Flint Cottage.

Then I went by bicycle to the Lobster Pot and found Donnie in. Together we went over the plans we had made. At least he had made them and I had consented. He kissed my unhappiness away. I promised I would help him bring the island to prosperity. It only wanted capital and I had that. What use to let my compensation moulder in a bank somewhere? It was mine and I could do what I liked with it. Best if I made it over to him, when we were man and wife. What was mine was his. We'd dredge the harbour and see to the jetty at the Isle. We'd put some new life into the fishing-fleet. We'd make the castle a comfortable home.

Back at Flint Cottage there was a letter from my guardian and a parcel delivered by hand. I took them to my cabin and glanced through the letter.

... it is important that I meet your prospective husband. With your permission, I will do this as soon as it can be arranged. There are legal details to be made and your marriage settlement arranged.

You have always thought me as aged. It was some misconception at the start, and I thought it best to let it stand. I am young enough to appreciate the problem that has come up. I know first-hand what youth and wildness can do to a young heart.

Robert out and my guardian in – Box and Cox. There was no time left, only a letter to write.

Dear Penny Box Man,

Thanks for your letter today. I am very sorry, but they forced my hand and I am of age. I can make my own decisions. I am no child. When I was, I planned to marry Robert Penn. Maybe I still loved him a bit, till I saw Donald Conningsby. I knew at first sight there

146

was nobody else for me. I'll not change, but meanwhile the cottage is misery and it's my doing. Gran has started to use any weapon to get her way. Last night she tried to make me believe that Len Marshall of the Lobster Pot had told her that Major Conningsby was a gambler and a drunk and a wrong 'un. She is so unsophisticated that she does not realise a gentleman may take wine with his dinner and lay a wager on the National. I will never listen to lies about him and I must, but what has happened to this home? I intend to present them with the accomplished fact.

Just now, I am a great disappointment to you all. I have wrecked the career that you had made possible. Forgive me for what I am doing now, and thank you for that bright golden future that might have been. Think happiness in your heart for me ...

I put the letter in my pocket and took out the parcel. Deep in the rustle of white tissue-paper was a replica of the Martello Tower in silver, beautifully wrought, engraved round the base.

THERE WILL BE NO PERSECUTION FOR HILLARY RUDD AT THE MARTELLO TOWER, ONLY THE WHITE GATE OPEN AND THE GANG-PLANK DOWN.

There was no time left to cry. Gran cornered me as I tried to creep through the sitting-room, and I had stowed the replica in my pocket with the letter. I took it out and showed it to her to avoid the other topic.

"Robert Penn's a better man than the one you've set your mind on," she said, jutting out her jaw.

She fumbled round till she found her glasses and set them

on her nose, and she looked at the replica for a long time. Then she handed it back to me, frowning at me over the gold rims.

"He's put his signature on it too in his own writing, and you haven't even seen that. I'll never know what that Nine-Pins accident did to you, but you're a changed girl – can't see that's in front of your nose. That man of yours said something that first day that turned me agen him – said I were too old maybe or something like that, but I remember well what young love was. With my Adam I'd have sailed the seven seas and wanted none other. Bless you, my darlin'. Mind how you goo."

I took the Tower from her and put it my pocket again, wrapped in the rustle of tissue-paper, walked past her and down Sea Lane, posted the letter to my guardian in the box. My heart was pounding against my ribs and my breath was short and shallow.

I caught the bus at the Main Road and got out at Narborough Tea Shop, not far from Hale's School.

Donnie's car was parked a little way along the street, by the War Memorial and Bert at the wheel, Donnie sitting in the back. Bert opened the rear door for me to get in.

"I never thought you'd come," Donnie said, and put his hand on my cheek briefly. "Even now, I don't know if we're right. If you like, I'll take you home and say good-bye. Let it all settle for a while. I've been wrong to make so much unhappiness for you. God knows, I'll have to be on my way back to the crofters, but I'd come back."

I pleaded with him to drive north. I knew that he had arranged the special licence. He had an appointment in a wee kirk for the ceremony. I had written to my bank manager to advise money in an account in a bank in Oban, Argyll, Scotland.

"Do as Miss Rudd says, Bert. Drive north."

When we were clear of Narborough, he took me in his arms and there was a look on his face that made me want to weep. He had a hunger for me and sadness – that uncared-for loneliness that haunted him. I knew I would spend the rest of my life making him happy, giving him all the things he had never had, like love and caring. He kissed my tears away and told me we would drive all night. We would stop in an hotel on the border and then we'd be in Scotland and away.

"Maybe 'they'll have swift steeds that follow'," he said.

That was young Lochinvar – and it figured.

I do not know what we ate in that small hotel. I had stopped looking over my shoulder. I had shut out Flint Cottage. I had left a letter. They would have found it by now.

We lazed across Scotland, and somewhere by a lonely loch we slept in each other's arms. Bert pulled the peak of his cap over his eyes and snored softly. We went right across England and Scotland, talking and sleeping. Then it was past and ended and we might have taken the road from Hale's School to come home to Marram for the holidays and it seemed no longer. We arrived, and here was the Atlantic and the Hebrides. We drew into the front drive of a big hotel where the hall porter came down the steps to greet us. Bert saw to the unpacking of the luggage, and we were at the reception-desk. We were expected, and 'Welcome to the Highlands and Islands'.

There were two single rooms booked for Major

Conningsby and Miss Rudd. A room for the Major's personal servant had been reserved adjacent to the Major's. The valet would dine in the staff quarters. I was not accustomed to such grandeur, and it impressed me.

He was such an honourable young man. 'His strength was as the strength of ten because his heart was pure.' Sir Galahad. There were red roses in my room from him. We must change and meet again over dinner.

His blue velvet dinner-jacket made his eyes so deep that I drowned with my love for him. We watched the four swans that swam in the sea beside the promenade, and he fetched bread from the hotel for me to feed them. Then at last he kissed my cheek and left me at my bedroom door, this honourable young man.

We had a Scots breakfast with baps, baked fresh. This was a land that would have pleased Gran. Afterwards we saw to business. The bank had transferred the money, and I spoke to the manager and told him about my forthcoming marriage and what I wanted done. We signed papers and he shook hands with us – looked after us as we walked off along the street. We had to be resident in Mull for a specified time, but it was all fixed.

Donnie's bank had slipped up. He had advised money on from Norwich, but it had been held up. He had gone in first thing, and he came back to the hotel to fetch me, dismayed, angry.

I slipped a note-case from my bag into his pocket and told him not to worry.

"I haven't even got the funds to pay our fare to 'the Isles'," he confessed. "I gave the manager hell. Bert and I made a night of it, after you were in your room last night. I'm spent up."

"It'll sort itself out. What's mine is yours now and you're free to draw on my credit anytime you like. You know you said we'd have a joint empire on Shona's Isle, and so we shall."

We sailed on the Island steamer to Mull and landed at a small town, drove the length of the coast to Tobermory and stopped half-way for a picnic. There were bottles of champagne packed in the boot and a case of whisky, and I knew where some of Donnie's money had gone. I was unsophisticated, not used to the luxury life. Yet Gran stood at my elbow with her 'gamblers and drunkards'. Bert seemed to spend a great deal of the day in betting-shops, but Donnie could never be classified as a wrong 'un.

It was the same sort of hotel in Tobermory as at Oban, the same room arrangements too. We stayed there for three nights and explored the Island by day. We planned what was to be done for Shona. I think, in that time, we reorganised the whole place and set the castle to rights, dredged the harbour, planned repairs to tenants' cottages, and set to yacht-varnishing the fishing-boats. Then the great day came, but we agreed that it was to be a very unofficial wedding. Donnie suggested it and I agreed, though it might have disappointed Gran with no white for the bride, nor yet 'something borrowed and something blue'. The kirk was small and very unprosperous. The parson was 'a church mouse' in a neatly darned cassock. The sexton and his wife 'stood up' as witnesses, for Bert had gone off to make a phone call and did not come back till too late. We signed the register and I had my marriage lines, and it was over.

If I was disappointed, it was soon put right. There was a surprise planned.

At a little quay somewhere, waited a man with a lobster-boat. He was to take Donnie and me to an island called Ruadh, which meant 'red' in Gaelic. It had so many rowan trees and their berries red! Bert was to follow in a few days with the car, but for the moment we would be alone. There was a small cottage, with the sea lapping its doorstep, and everything had been laid on. A local girl would see after the work and the cooking, and Donnie and I would explore the mountain, which had a great surprise in the very summit. We must not pretend we were newly married. If we did the Scots would expect celebrations and the skirlin' of pipes, and that must happen on Shona's Isle 'with our ain folk'.

It was like Alice in Wonderland and Walt Disney rolled into one. The cottage was just right for the Seven Dwarfs and Snow White and there was an unreality about the perfection of the ocean and the mountains that stood all about. We even had our own particular hill at the back, rising straight from the cottage, and the islands scattering the Atlantic with beauty.

The lobster-fisherman had taken us across at his own pace and laid his pots as he went, but he asked our permission first. He winked at Donnie and wished us a good time, and then went off about his business.

We looked at the cottage, and the Scots girl introduced herself as Fiona Stuart. Her mother was 'the post' in the town.

Donnie must have it that we went walking off up the hill at once. This was no time for resting. There was the surprise, that was the best of all still to come. Fiona spoke Gaelic. They all did, but she had the English too. She would set the supper out ready for us. There was no hurry

152

to get back. It was a lovely view from the mountain and we must take care to see that the island was all quicken trees, and by that she meant rowans.

It was a tough climb and it might have been wiser if we had picked tougher shoes, but I was still in a smart London town outfit and my feet were too fashionable. There were rowans in plenty and gorse in great glorious stretches, so that I thought it might be called a golden isle. We scuffed deep through the heather, and the bracken was beginning to shoot light green growth.

"Now for the surprise," said Donnie when we reached the flat plateau on the very top and I was trying to take in the enormity of the view. There was a small island to the west, not far away, sheltered in the lee of Ruadh.

"There's Shona's Isle. It's yours."

I was quite speechless and just stood and looked and could not believe. It was a miniature of any Scots island, but such care had been taken of it by nature and by the hand of man. The castle was small and noble. There were small mountains and hills – sheep on them with lambs, little patchwork fields with cocks of hay, Highland cattle roaming free.

The harbour was Marram, but the fisher-folk might have been from light opera. They were dressed in pink bobbled caps and high-necked sweaters to match. The boats certainly needed no repairs.

"There's your surprise. I knew I could never describe why I love it, and you'll love it too. Maybe I wanted to prove that I'm not marrying you for all that money you have, but you have something I want more than any money in the world."

153

He took me into his arms and drew me down to the soft moss of the mountain. He whispered to me softly and sweetly, and he caressed me and soon with no gentleness at all. It was like the wedding. It was not what I had planned, and I thought of the night-dress still in my luggage. There was pain, and I thought to come to pleasure, but gorse was not any good for making love. There was too much of it. It would be better soon. We were man and wife, and there were long years to come. There was a big goose-feather bed at the foot of the hill in the cottage. I started to laugh, and laughed till I cried, and wondered if my shoes would take me as far, or if I might be better to try the descent in my bare feet. Yet we were very happy on our way down to the sea, and the world seemed the same rose-spectacled place as it had been the day we met.

We explored Ruadh on foot and messed about in a boat that was at the cottage. Bert arrived at the quay in the town three days later, and we went in to meet him and were glad to have the luxury of the car and Bert again. For one thing, Bert improved the living standard in the cottage, and he was company for Donnie. Maybe 'the Don', as Bert called him, had missed his valet. Now the food was served perfectly and the wine and spirits flowed freely. There were nights when they both disappeared and Fiona was left to serve me a fish I had caught from the sea. They would come home very late from a walk across Ruadh, but I knew they had been in some inn. Donnie would fall into bed and asleep at once. I had to fetch Bert to him one night because I thought he might be ill, but after he had vomited he seemed better.

Again, Gran materialised by the bed with 'drunkards

and gamblers and wrong 'uns', but I sent her about her business.

I began to suspect that they avoided my company sometimes. They would go fishing, and be gone before I could go with them; and again would come one of these nights when I had supper alone and Fiona telling me that all men were the same.

Bert was a great trial to Fiona for he was determined to 'lay' her. I overheard him say so to Donnie and was astonished that Donnie laughed.

"She runs too fast for you, old man. You'll not catch her, you dirty old bastard. She's young enough to be your daughter. For Christ's sake, don't muck up everything when we're nearly through."

We were there three weeks, when Donnie became uneasy. The money from his bank should have arrived. He went in and collected the letters when they brought them from the mainland in the ferry, but always there was nothing. His anger mounted.

He might be classified as a kept man. He refused to live on me any more and he was going to chase down that bank manager in Oban. He had contrived a master plan. It was time we were home on Shona anyhow, so he would take the car and Bert and the ferry. They could cross to Oban and tackle the bank man. If necessary they would have transport to Glasgow or Inverness. He'd see the matter over and done, and I was not to worry my head over it. It was so easy to arrange. All the luggage would be packed and they'd be back in two to three days. I'd have only a light case. I must be waiting for the ferry at Ruadh town. I would jump aboard her, and in no time at all we'd be

155

disembarking on the Isle of Shona, and the bagpipes would start skirling ...

I held out against it. I was being left behind.

"You'll have to rest. You've no idea what you'll have to face on Shona. Fiona will see after you, but don't talk to her too much. Every word you say will be all over Ruadh. Her mother's 'the post'."

I saw them off at the ferry and came home to an empty house – it was a desolate place. I confided in Fiona about the money having been mislaid and she laughed at me.

"Why wad he fret aboot siller with the big car and the lovely rich lassie and a man to wait on him – that old man wi' the squintin' e'en. I can't abide him. The maister makes too much of him."

The feather bed was peopled with nightmares in the empty cottage. The bad dreams came, when villains crept up the stairs and tried the door-handle. I was up and waiting for Fiona to come in the morning. The cottage seemed deserted, for everything was packed and in the boot of the car.

I had got out the silver tower and put it on the mantelpiece that was made from granite carried up from the shore. It was a steadying factor in my life. Robert Penn had sent it. I missed him sorely. Only to myself I confessed that the feather bed held a terrible secret. I could never reveal it, that I had found little joy there. Then I had maybe committed the unforgivable sin. I had imagined Robert Penn lay with me and I had known such ecstasy, so I had wronged my husband and there was *no* forgiveness for me, unless I put it down here now. Gran would have whipped me at the tail of a cart through Marram, but it was done innocently in a dream. How could I turn off dreams?

The second day I walked into Ruadh town. They even had rowan trees in the little square near the quay, where the Post Office shop stood, with a scattering of crofts and hens running free and a Jersey cow, that came up to talk to me. I chatted to the fishermen down at the quay, and they said the 'ferry wad be in the morn'. We had a common interest in the sea, and I got on fine with them. They showed me the lifeboat, and they seemed to like me, but I knew but half of what they said.

I walked up the small slope into the Post Office shop. There were two customers there, and all the talk stopped. Fiona's mother was Scots, Scots, Scots, just the same sort of character as Gran. I was homesick for Gran.

"Don't be putting ideas in Fiona's head," she said when the customers had gone. I looked at her in surprise.

"I don't think you know who I am. I'm Major Conningsby's wife and he's laird of Shona."

I heard her call to her husband that she thought I was daft as I went down the glen with my post cards and a tin of sardines – and I was in cloud-cuckoo land again.

Then I was back at the cottage with Fiona, and I had to be up early in the morning to meet the ferry. Fiona was in the cottage waiting for me to come from Ruadh Post, and she avid for gossip, but Donnie had told me not to talk.

"I did na think the Major was coming back at all. I'm sorry that I had it that you were na wed. I did na understand why my Pa had agreed to wait for the money, but I was afraid to say it to him. That old man wi' the squinting e'en was evil, and he was hand-in-glove wi' his boss. He told me that the Major had a wife in every port

157

and drew siller from them all, but I knew that was sailor's talk. I clouted Bert on the lug, and I could rin too fleet. I had an idea in my heid that you were in strange company, Mistress, and you're not too strong to your health. Maybe the Major makes good siller out of the rich women, I thought to mysel', and herself's rich," she said.

I was too horrified to take her seriously. This was a strange place, with unreality in every part of it. I managed to grin at her and told her she had been seeing too much piped T.V.

"There are them that strangle their wives in the act of love," she said. "I saw the marks on your throat."

That brought me up sharp. Donnie could be rough.

"Mind how you walk, Mistress Conningsby. They say you're a rich lady and there are folk ..."

"You've got a rich imagination," I laughed. "You're talking poppycock."

"I don't know rightly what is poppycock, but if they're not on the boat tomorrow I daresay you'll pay Pa."

I nodded my head, told her not to worry, and thanked her for all she had done for me.

"I couldn't have survived the last days without you, Fiona, though we did make a mess of the grate with the barbecue."

"Barbecue and poppycock," Fiona said. "Isn't it a strange tongue the English have? A body wouldn't understand one half that's said. There are times when I think it isn't this time of the year at all, but you're a bonnie wife ..."

She took herself off, and there was this strange unreality again. I wondered if she were the daft one. It rained all night. It was still raining the soft mist in the morning when

Fiona's father collected me and my overnight case in the trap. Fiona had arrived earlier, and we had had breakfast and tidied the cottage. I was very excited at the thought of meeting the ferry, looking forward to my embarkation for Shona's Isle, and the mists of all doubts shining to happiness. I thought that the fishermen and their families might be gathered to meet us on Shona's quay. Then quite suddenly I wondered how the ferry could come in to Shona's Isle. These were doubts that would not go away. I could not bring myself to ask Fiona or her father. There was no ramp in that small harbour ... Fiona's father was so very solicitous about me, and he had covered us in against the rain with an old tarpaulin. He started to talk about the island that lay to the west, and there was embarrassment in him. Then he said it was no matter, that it was no business of his and kept silent.

I was standing on the landing-stage in Ruadh town at last, and the ship almost docked. A great relief came to me. Fiona and her father stayed close by, but I hardly noticed them. Soon he would be here and I in his arms again. The ship was sliding in and the ramp was going down for the cars. There was no sign of Donnie at the rail, so he must be in the car. A Land-Rover drove off first, then a jeep, and that was all, a few passengers coming ashore, a few going aboard, but then of course the car would not have come ashore. We must go on to Shona. I ran aboard and went looking for them, but they were not to be found. There was no familiar car. I sought out the purser and asked, but there was nobody of that name on board, not booked with a car.

Fiona's father had followed me, and he took my arm in his, led me back to the staging, his face anxious.

"I think ye made a mistake in Shona's Isle," he said.

159

"Mistress Isobel McTavish hae ruled it for years, and she's an elderly body. She'll hae naebody set a foot on it. Maybe she thinks it's a dollies' housie, the way she dresses her folk up in pink Shetland wool, the best to be got. She's no' marrit. She's no gradh for sex of any sort. She'll not hae a dog on the island, for she rins a wee bitch in the castle."

There was no sense in anything. The steamer had started to move away from the quay. The grey mist rolled in from the sea and wrapped her from view, and her siren moaned.

There might be a dozen reasons why he had not come – just missed the ferry perhaps, or had an accident. He might still be in Glasgow or Inverness and delayed, yet why was Shona's Isle not ours? The mist was coming in my head. Why had Fiona thought that he was not coming back? Why had Fiona thought I was having an affair? Why had there been all the small mean doubts? Gran had said Donnie was a wrong 'un. Had she really said that? Had she? Had they been right -- and had I been wrong?

I woke in the parlour of the Post Office.

"Are ye better, Mistress Conningsby? For a whilie ye' were real poorly."

I gathered my wits together as best I could, but they scattered like sheep. It was a fearful nightmare. Then I was in the swirling cold waves of the North Sea and the two dogs with me. Rouge was rolling under the water and I grabbed at her cable, recognised it was all over, the dream.

"Tak' it doon in the one gulp," said a voice in my ear.

They had given me fire to drink. It lit me from head to toe, burnt me up like a flame-thrower. Then my mind began to clear.

"The ferry does na ca' at Shona's Isle, and if the Major told ye he owned Shona's Isle he was telling ye false."

"I think I've been a fool," I whispered. "I want help badly, or think I do. My folks are a long way away. Could you help me, as if I were Fiona, if I told you? I can't see clearly what to do ..."

Mrs. Stuart's voice was calm and comforting, but what she said was alarming enough.

"My brother-in-law is the Polis on Ruadh. He's at home, for he's been out after the feshing. If you'd allow me to fetch him in? I think it's a job for the Polis, but he's a chap that can keep a still mouth. We guard our tongues on Ruadh."

Police Sergeant Stuart held my wedding-certificate in his hands. For all his kindly official look his only regulation police dress was his trousers. His gear otherwise was the dress of the men of Marram. Right enough, he had been out after fish. What was more, he knew of Marram lifeboat, the *Adam, Seth and Joshua Rudd*. He had heard of yon daft wee lassie that had jumped into a stormy sea after twa dogs ...

The Stuart family, God bless them, took me to their hearts.

The Sergeant went to phone, and was back presently.

"You're man and wife right enough, Mrs. Conningsby. The ceremony was legal and every condition was carried out. Both birth-certificates were in order and all the papers were filled and registered in law."

He looked at me and shook his head sadly, asked if I was up to ringing Major Conningsby's bank in Oban, the place he might have gone two days past.

I sat on a high stool at the telephone in the 'Post', and there was a woman on the line in Donnie's bank. I knew I might be making a fuss about nothing. Yet fear had rushed in on me.

"Major Donald Conningsby, did ye say? He was in two,

161

three days past. Ye'd be best speaking wi' the manager."

I could hear her footsteps retreating, and after a long time, more steps on the tiles, coming back.

"This is Mr. Fife on the line. Did ye say Major Conningsby, a dark gentleman? Aye, he said a lady might call – Mrs. Conningsby, née Rudd. I daresay that's yourself on the line, and I'm glad tae meet you. I have a wee note to post tae ye, but the Ferry's away and we had na' the envelope typed ready. I'll see it's on the next steamer going that way."

He had all the time in the world. There was a leisure about him that I seemed to have lost for ever.

"I'll be obliged if you'd open it and read it out to me."

There was a tearing of the envelope flap.

"It's only a wee note. My! He writes a fine bold hand, Mistress. It says, I quote,

"Good bye, Hillary, dear Hillary Rudd. Thanks for everything. If things had been different maybe I'd have been different. As it is, we shan't meet again. I'm on my way south to the Med to find the sun. Count the last weeks as a sweet dream. Debit them to experience ..."

I had copied the words down and I passed them to Sergeant Stuart.

On the phone I managed to thank the manager and tell him I might call for the note myself. If I did not, I promised to post him an address for it to be forwarded. I could not recognise my own voice.

Back in the parlour the Sergeant was a terrier on the track of a rat.

"It's a confidence trick," he said. "Ring yer ain bank in Oban this minute. It's past time ye did. We want evidence, but I daresay we're too late."

I looked at him blankly, and he almost shouted at me, hurried to get the number for me when he had asked me which bank.

"Cancel the order you gave for it to be a joint account. Cancel the order ye gave for your property to be transferred to your husband. Cancel everything you did and block all cheques. Och! Ma puir wee lassie ..."

I took the phone from his hand, and he had the line in Oban. He had some delay in getting the manager for the bank was shut and the manager was almost through the door and on his way home to Pulpit Hill. The Sergeant electrified the financial world, and by the time I spoke to him the manager was as worried as the law. I got it said, what I wanted to say.

"It's too late," he cried. "Your husband called two days ago. He checked that the transaction with our branch was terminated. You recall your man could sign on your behalf. The credit is no business of ours any more. It's been transferred. Maybe we can block further cheques, but I doubt it. It's my advice that you should contact your solicitor this very moment, but the man has done nothing illegal. You gave him full power. You gave him, of your own free will. You did it in front of my eyes. If you're legally his wife, there's nothing you can do. Put the phone down now and get in touch with your solicitor and maybe your stock-broker too, but ye signed yourself awa'. It's no good to go running to the Polis. It's a domestic matter."

My mind was at the top of a canting green sward, that I would roll down and end up in the rearing white horses again. There was a great wave coming up and it would

destroy me, yet I recognised the old nightmare. I grabbed
Skippy by the scruff of the neck and I turned my eyes from
looking out to sea. I could feel the graze of the concrete and
the drenched grass of the dunes. What was Mr. Tulliver's
address? It drifted in on the tide and I managed to find the
phone somewhere in all the flotsam.

I gave the girl at the exchange the number and had it
more quickly than Oban, but Mr. Tulliver was not in. I
dictated the message to his secretary – private and
confidential. It was too late, but all my financial deals must
be stopped. My message would have to be solved, but Mr.
Tulliver would understand it.

"Keep Marram out of it completely, unless you advise
not. I will contact you ..."

I put down the phone and knew that there was nothing
more I could do. I seemed not to care if I was penniless. It
was the treachery of Donnie that reduced me to an old rag
doll all over again. I wished I had died in the Nine-Pin
Tragedy. I had trusted him. I had loved him. I had been
consumed in the firestorm of my passion, and all the time
he had been taking me for my money. He had taken me
with as much love as he might have taken a whore. He must
have joked about it with Bert when they were alone
together. I had hated it, and now I could say it. It had been
cruel.

Back with the Sergeant, I managed to hold myself in
order. I told him what I had done in my arrangements, and
he nodded his head.

"I doot if he'll be able to dae anything, Mistress. This
situation is one that we get a time or two, but you had a
trust in your husband that was agen us. He cud hae faked

that wedding, but he did na dae it. Maybe you did na let him make free wi' you, but maybe he wanted it secure, that we cud na give evidence agen ye. Then to nail everything, you gave him your fortune. Lock, stock and barrel. He can do whit he pleases wi' it and ye canna give evidence agen him, I tell ye noo, whit he'll say. He'll say it's a domestic tiff. We canna even go looking for him. He'd be all innocent. He has nae broken the law ... just has na found ye tae his taste. It's all loaded agen ye, no matter if he's spent every penny he's had off ye. Ye giv' it to him, out of the love that was in your hairt."

He paused and shook his head.

"If you want him found, the Salvation Airmy will dae it, but they will na tell ye where he is, only if he lets them tae dae it. That's the law."

He advised me to go home 'to Coxswain Rudd', but this I could not do yet – not bring all this trouble down on Flint Cottage.

They made sure I had enough money to take me home. Then they left me by the fire for a sleep. I had money in my night-bag. I checked it. There was a pocket in the lid of the case, and Donnie had not known about it. I kept my 'emergency' cash there, and had enough and to spare. Donnie had 'taken' the Stuart family too. They would not hear of accepting payment for our debts. I left notes behind the clock – planned one day, when this was all over, to send them more. In the case I found the Martello Tower model, and I held it against my breast and was home. The light was bright in the Hebrides. The Tower shone more than I had ever seen it shine. I turned it over idly to see if it was hall-marked, and then I saw the signature, but it was not like Robert Penn's signature. Anyway, he always signed himself Robert. You could read Robert well enough, but then there was a squiggle and a skidding line down to the edge of the rim. I had seen it before at the end of every one of my guardian's letters, for years and years and years. Gran had known about the signature. She had mocked me because I had not noticed it. I had not known that my mysterious guardian had always been Robert Penn. He had been the confidant of every innermost secret I had since my adolescence. He had cared for me. He had devoted his life to me. There was a time when I had loved him, and I loved him still. Slowly the fact trickled into my mind. I loved Robert Penn deeply and tenderly. Donald Conningsby had been a firestorm, and the flames had all burnt out. I was a fool who had been taken for everything I had, and there was nothing I could do about it.

8

THE SEA-GULL

They left me to rest, alone in the parlour before the peat fire in the Post Office. Mistress Stuart had letters to deliver across the island from the ferry. The men kind were for the fishing. I had the house to myself. For all I knew I had the little town to myself, so quiet it was. I must have slept, for I had been sitting as miserably as David Copperfield's mother had sat before her parlour fire on the day before David was born. Aunt Betsy Trotwood's face had pressed against the window and startled her, but it was different in my case, for there was a soft tap first and then the face of the Penny Box. Yet I knew well that my Penny Box at this moment stood on the mantelshelf in Flint Cottage. I saw the face, square, honest, friendly, black sou'wester, greying beard, pipe between his teeth. His eyes roamed the room to search for me – found me. He pointed towards the door of the Post Office and I went round to open it to him. It seemed that Mistress Stuart had said I was in haste to get to Oban. Did I mind a speedy boat?

I shook my head.

"The ferry's not due for two days. I've had a call for lobsters for the West Highland in Oban. Mr. Fingland

167

wants them by supper-time, and he's a strict man. I have them ready for the table, and they're packed in the stern. They won't worry you if you're Noah Rudd's girl. I can have you in Oban in time for the night train, and you can be home quickly. Mistress Stuart asked me before she went off up the mountain, said to slip you out on the tide. If you're Hillary Rudd I'm proud to be taking your hand."

I had a feeling as if I was being kidnapped. There was nobody around in the village. The fleet was at sea. The speedboat was moored and 'Noah Rudd will see things right in Marram'. The kindly fisherman smiled and picked up my case.

"But keep a still tongue."

I had just looked in the case and seen the silver tower. I had found Mary Canning's letter, too, that had followed me to the Islands on my honeymoon. I had read it and had forgotten it. Now I remembered what it said. Mary was on holiday. She was taking a lone holiday on the Broads, on the old *Elros* – a Norfolk inland holiday on a watercraft we had called 'the old hulk', where she and I had once had a holiday. Now she was expecting to go there again to unwind. The life in hospital was killing her.

It was not for some time yet, but if this letter found me I must come running. The letter was all behind time, but time had caught up with it. She was due in Norfolk in the future, but the future was the present.

Mary Canning was in Norfolk now. I knew the place well, and there was a welcome waiting. She could not know what trouble I was in. The dates of her holiday were printed in blocks. There it was – loud and clear. I had only to go to the place where the *Elros* was always moored.

The Sea-Gull

I decided not to go to Marram. I must have a little time to sort things out. The boat was skimming the sea, catching the rise of the Atlantic from one wave-crest to the next. Maybe my courage regenerated a bit. The mist had lifted from the mountains and the lobster-boats were scattered between the islands. The fisherman had no word to say to me, but he took me to Oban as swiftly and surely as any Scots fisherman could have done it.

"Away to the railway station and a still tongue remember," he said. "Give my regards to Noah Rudd. Tell him that he has no need of a son, with the fine daughter he has."

He waved aside all my thanks, wheeled the craft about and was off to the promenade pier. There had been a time when Donnie and I had watched the swans, sailing in the evening, but it was all past now.

I was aboard the train, and it moved out on the hour. I made my plans as we crossed the Highlands. It was a long journey and there is no point in describing it. We left the islands behind, said good bye to the mountains and the heather – went on and on. Then after a long time Scotland was left behind and the border was breached, and *Haste ye Back*, and soon it was a stern busy life. Then off away towards Lincolnshire and over The Wash and on – and flat country. Here was Norfolk, and maybe a century past – and I knew the train and the bus and the walk along a towpath somewhere in the Broads. I found the drift that ran along a slow river, but I had reached it by bus. Time had ceased to mean much – only that if I were lucky I would find Mary Canning waiting. It was quite impossible that all my hoping could ever turn to reality. The twilight was coming down when I sighted the *Elros*, unchanged from the last time. We had said it might have belonged to 'the Great Mogul', who-ever he might be. We had laughed a great deal, three years ago, at the oriental splendour on the Broads of this one craft.

Mary Canning was sitting out top with a fishing-line, faded wind-cheater, disreputable jeans. She had fallen asleep, and there was an eel on her line making a tangle. She woke up and saw me, rubbed her eyes and looked again, and her face lit up to sunshine the dying day.

"Hillary Rudd," she yelled at the top of her voice. "Hillary Rudd, the miracle of modern surgery. God! Look at my bloody line! It's in a hell of a mess."

We untangled the line and let the eel go free. I wished it might be as easy to untangle me. Then we sat down to the first meal I had enjoyed for days. Mary had gone racing like a hare along the river-bank, back in twenty minutes with an armful of fish and chips, warm, newspaper-wrapped, salted and soused with vinegar. It was all the midnight feasts at Hale's of Narborough rolled into one. I told her my story as we ate. With the darkness down all about us and the willows not reflecting in the clear water any more, we started our plans, stretched out one on either bunk and mighty glad to be together again.

"So you married 'a flim-flam man' and you married him legally. Were you out of your mind?"

"I think he must have deceived a great many women ..."

"He won't deceive any more," Mary ground out between her teeth. "God! When I think of Marram and that family of yours, never injured anybody, and this chap and his accomplice have the nerve to destroy Flint Cottage – for

170

that's just what they've done. We've got a first priority, honey. We've got to run down these villains, even if the police can't put a finger on them legally. We've got to see that they go out of business, sharpish. There must be something."

"I'll go home soon to Flint Cottage," I said. "I scrawled a note to Gran, said I'd be by soon, nothing else – sent it on from some big town yesterday morning."

"That won't do," Mary told me. "I'll visit Marram. God knows I've stayed there enough times. I'll just drop in. You stay here and rest till I get back with the set-up. God knows how much they know or don't know."

The next day Mary set off for Marram, and I sorted out all the cleaning materials. I got the brass shining and the boards scrubbed white, but it was a long day. She came back after dark when I had quite given her up, and she was as bright as the brass.

"I won't open my mouth till I'm filled with rashers and eggs," she said. "That Marram Mob must have been smugglers in past generations. They have a plan, and the watchword is 'Watch the wall, my darling, while the gentlemen go by'. That's Kipling's Smugglers' song."

When she had had her bacon and eggs, she told me that the news had not been broken in Marram yet. Only the family, and that included herself, knew all that had happened – Robert Penn too.

"For all anybody knows at Marram you're still on your honeymoon in the Hebrides, but the Marram Mob have it all. They have worked out a plan, and you and I are to keep clear of it. Your husband and his 'batman' have come south. They're hanging about Yarmouth mostly, but they're watching Flint Cottage and the Martello Tower – no car, no publicity, just waiting.

"Gran was more than relieved to know that you were with me, but her instructions are quite definite. We're to have no part in what's to be done. It's all fixed, and we'd only complicate things."

There was plenty to hear, and I listened. Robert Penn had been on to Donald Conningsby and Bert from the start. When I flit from Marram, he was already in London, where he had contacts. There was an Inspector in Scotland Yard, a friend of his, and he had the entrée to the Yard unofficially. There was no good wondering how it was done. Robert wrote detective fiction, and he got an unofficial look at 'mug-shot' files. He picked the two villains without much delay. They were confidence tricksters. They had both done time. They were quite well known and they would never reform. They had a string of women like a harem left behind them …"

The trouble was this time, they had not broken the law.

"You're Mrs. Conningsby, and you've given him everything of your own free will. That man can come walking down the bank there now and claim his conjugal rights – demand you to set up house with him. The mystery is why they're still after you. Presumably they got your money and have it stashed away. Gran has her own ideas, but won't say a word. She fizzed with excitement every time she quoted the Smugglers' Song."

Mary took a letter out of her pocket and gave it to me, told me Gran had written it and that I was not to cry all over it, so I had best not read it yet.

"There's some more for you to hear first and it's about

Commander Penn. You'd best recall what they taught us in Hale's about history and legend ..."

She was very awkward about this part. It was Pygmalion – and Galatea. She had cast Penn as Pygmalion, she said, and failed to make it sound funny. He had carved a perfect woman in stone and had loved her so much that she had turned to life.

"You were Galatea," she said. "It's a God-awful job to tell you this. He had this girl that saved his dog, and had done a pretty good job. He got it into his head to give her the best education he could think of. He sent you to Hale's and up to Wentbridge. After the Nine-Pin Tragedy he still held fast to the idea, and he fell in love. You were in love with him too. Then this criminal and his mate must have seen about the immense damages awarded to you in the courts, and they set for you. It was their way of conning women, *modus operandi*. Each time they did it – watched the papers and went out like wolves to charm poor pretty rich injured ladies, grab their money and scarper. They've got your money. What do they want now? It's rather frightening."

"That's how it was done," I said, thinking of how Donnie had waited at the harbour that day. "I swear to you, Mary, you took one look at him and he was any super-star, and it wasn't that he pursued me. I swear I pursued him, but afterwards I began to have doubts. They were all so against me. I set my mind on having my own way. I forgot that I had decided to marry Robert. I never really thought much about Donnie, only that I must not be forced into the notion of marrying the Commander, because Gran had chosen him. I knew they all had and they thought I was a child."

173

I opened Gran's letter.

Little Fish, don't you be frightened at what lies ahead. Our love for you is something that villains have to reckon with. Robert Penn is still your guardian, and in a way so am I – was from the night you were put into my arms. Mary will have told you the news, but just lay low. They've missed something, but they'll regret they come back. We know what must be done, but don't come here or to the Martello, unless a message comes – with the password too. We know exactly what's happening. The storm will blow itself out. Nobody will even hear the wind ... Trust us in Flint Cottage and the store of pride we have for you ...

"Why are they still after me?" I murmured to Mary, and again she tried to make light of it by suggesting that they were going to take us both 'to play with the gypsies in the wood' – and the joke fell flat.

"I wasn't afraid in the old days," I said.

"You're as good a woman as ever you were," she scoffed. "You've had a hell of a time. I know there's nothing to this. The Marram Mob will recruit some of the lifeboat crew and they will give these bastards a hammering and send them off ... Just get it into your head that we're not to interfere. They'll clear off and we'll never hear from them again and maybe they'll think twice about crime."

"Gran might get killed," I muttered, and Mary laughed at that, and we both felt cheered.

"I'd be more inclined to think that Gran might kill the wrong 'uns."

I had lost every bit of the attraction of flame that had been what Donnie had held for the moth that was myself.

When I saw the full story, I was sickened how I had behaved so. It made me as miserable as I had ever been, and I knew myself second-hand goods. Infatuation was tinsel. It was gilt. I had put myself to shame. I imagined the conversations that Donnie and 'Bert' would have had 'behind my back.' There was no recovering such blows to one's pride.

"But nobody in Marram knows it," Mary said twenty times a day. "You're a legally married woman and you've split up or will split up when we settle what he's after. It's only a matter of having patience. Forget it."

The days passed slowly, and it was good of Mary to sit out the vigil with me. We were getting increasingly worried and frightened as one day slipped into another. Then the month was running out. The fogs set in and the dampness took over the *Elros*. Matches would not strike, and the breath of the mist was wet on the bulkhead. One night, what I think was a stray dog jumped into our dinghy, and we dared not move, just lay silent till whatever it was went away.

We became increasingly affected with this menace that threatened us. Mary confessed that she had the feeling that there was something wrong in Marram, and immediately she told me I had the same conviction.

"Remember the time we had Hallow E'en at Hale's. We were good at disguise. We got away with it then." I said.

"It's Hallow E'en tomorrow night," said Mary.

We had celebrated the night when witches fly. It had been the most wonderful trick of them all, and now it was of the same stuff as tinsel and infatuation and nonsense, for all that it might have got us both expelled. We had dressed up.

Mary had been disguised as one of the house-boys and I was one of the domestic helps. It had all seemed wonderful. We borrowed the clothes and then we set out boldly through the front gates of Hale's, hand-in-hand. We strolled the length of Narborough High Street to a fish and chip shop in a back lane, ordered 'fish and chips twice', sprinkled the salt and dashed on the vinegar. We went very slowly home to Hale's eating the feast in our hands, and then at last put the newspaper in a rubbish-bin on a lamp-post and licked our fingers all the way back through the gates and up the avenue.

There seemed no purpose in it now, only as a dress rehearsal.

I grabbed Mary by the arm.

"I know there's danger and I know it's on Hallow E'en. Tomorrow night I'm not going to sit here and let them come to harm at home. If you come with me we'll fight my battles together."

"Tomorrow evening then."

Mary was rummaging the boat. I found a black sweater, black wind-cheater, jeans to match and headscarf land in my lap. She found a check pair of trews and a green sweater for herself – a white muffler in lieu of tie. There was no cap that might suit a boy till she went along the bank and across a field and robbed a scarecrow – tried to find humour and found none, only fear.

"It's against all orders," she reminded me, and I told her I did not care. It was my responsibility, if they were hurt in Marram.

God knows what we did in the morning, but we were ready to go in time for the bus. We secured the boat and set off along the bank, but there were geese over our graves. I was glad when we came to the dirt road and then to a small country lane. There was a bus coming along and we flagged it down, thankful that it stopped for us.

"Ye cut it fine, Bor," said the Conductor. "Young 'uns is all the same. I hope ye're not late for your own funerals."

It was a long way to the turn off to Marram, but at last it came. The dusty road was so familiar that my heart started to thump in my chest. We kept to the lanes and out of sight – were relieved that the moon stayed hidden too. We had decided the course of action. Mary was to go to Flint Cottage and see they were all safe there. I was to go in the back way through the coppice to the Martello Tower. Mary knew well that I would have given my right arm to have a chance at seeing Robert Penn on my own. We had the slim excuse that we had been worried about them. It did not sound true. Mary disappeared along Sea Lane like a shadow, and for a moment I saw the lights of home and almost envied her. Then it was time to find the coppice ... It was much bigger, than I remembered it and very dark. I clawed my way through it like a herd of elephants, with the thought that there might be somebody behind me every step who had waited and stalked me, knowing that I must come. I had almost given up finding the Tower when I came on the bulk of it, and the trees were at an end. The Tower was lit up with every light it possessed, or so it seemed. The Rolls was parked out towards the cliff, where it sometimes stood in the dip. If Robert left it there, intending to go out again, he always backed down a yard and then swept it round in a great curve through the white gates. Here was the back door. The surface of it was wet

177

and clammy, and I caught my hand on rose-thorns. I knocked very softly and waited, and heard nothing but the beat of my own heart. I tried again, and scratched my hand again. Then I was full of fear and hammered on the wood with my fist and almost wept to be let in. Instantly the door was flung open and Robert Penn was silhouetted against the light, but if I expected a welcome it was not here. He looked at me as if he could not believe I stood there. Then he caught me by the shoulder and dragged me inside, shook his head, shut the door behind, but very quietly.

"You were told not to come here," he said. "You were given definite instructions. Why can you never do what you're told? You arrive here tonight of all nights. God above! What can I do with you!" He looked about him helplessly and then seized my hand and noticed the blood from the thorns, wrapped his handkerchief about the scratches, then grabbed my other hand and took me up the stairs at double speed to the galley. In ten seconds we were in the galley and he had flicked the curtains closed, snapped the light off. We stood in the darkness, face to face, and only the sound of our heavy breathing.

"Why had you to come tonight?" he demanded. "God knows I've hoped you'd come a hundred nights, but you never came. They're on their way here this minute. Your husband telephoned me a while ago. I'm expecting him with his man now. You'll have to stay in here and not a sound out of you ..."

He went on as if he did not know what to say, just as if he waited out an interval.

"The brake is gone on the car. The tide's full tonight. Jimma Grimes is to fix the car first thing tomorrow. Why must everybody come calling tonight? There's danger all about us ..."

"Mary Canning went to Flint Cottage," I said. "We wanted to find out if they were all well there?"

"Did she indeed?" he demanded, and did some fine cursing.

"Something's upset your husband's plans. We don't know why. There's no doubt they're after you and they mustn't find you."

He searched round the darkness of the galley for his pipe and found it, though he sent some crockery crashing to the deck with an almighty smash. Then the struck match lit up the room, and he found his tobacco. His hand shook as he filled the pipe, and that angered him.

"Dear Penny Box Man!" I whispered. "What's going on?"

"It's better if you know nothing," he said.

"I came to see if you were safe," I whispered. "I wanted to thank you, for you gave me the world and I threw it away. I never recognised the signature and I should have known that the guardian's typewriter was yours. Gran knew. She told Mary the other day. She knew who you were."

"She's not been through what you've been through," he said. "Down there tonight I was astonished to see you've put on all your armour again, bloody with the rose-thorns, same Copper."

"I was supposed to watch the wall," I said, and he spun me round to face the curtains.

"It's as safe a place as any," he said, and I thought he had laughed a little, but if he did it was switched off.

He went on almost to himself.

"Conningsby's a con-man, but you'll know that the hard way by now. He was a child in a Home and they farmed him out to a public school as a house-boy, so he got the manners, got the military habits from the O.T.C. His job was cleaner in the school chapel. He made a career from his imitations of life, didn't realise that men aren't all captains and kings and majors, but you know that too."

All men would have had the same judgement, but a foolish woman would have let him go free.

"Nobody will ever change recidivists. The 'Don' and his friend watch the papers for accident cases that get big damages, and then they go in. They collect the damages and then, maybe, blackmail, too. They have a fool-proof set-up, and this time you played into their hands. You made it all legal. He rang me tonight, told me quite openly that he was coming here, and he'll come, and you'll stay put quietly. He won't get away with it, not this time. If ever you do anything, you're advised to do, don't make a sound. Leave him to us, and don't ever run away from me again. I love you."

I promised him I would hide out, but not only in the galley. I would hide out for the rest of my life. I would hide out from Marram for the shabbiness of what had happened, from him, from everybody."

"Oh, no," he said, and again, "Oh, no."

There was a sound on the front drive, and he put his lips against my ear.

"Watch the wall, my darling. The gentlemen are about to arrive, but they're not our gentlemen. They're on the wrong side."

180

He was gone, and I was facing the curtains still and there was no doubt of the loud knocking at the front door. Robert's footsteps were light on the stairs and the door opened.

"Conningsby," he said. "And Bert too."

I had turned round from the curtain and opened the door a sliver. I looked down on a view of the whole lovely central living-room, the shaded lights, the spiral staircase to the roof, the white rope hand-rail.

Robert must have helpers standing by. Where were they? He had admitted his guests, and he seemed quite calm about it. His pipe had gone out, and he put it down on the glass table beside the key-ring with the semi-precious red stone that held the car keys. The stone shone brightly – red – red – red.

Conningsby awaited no invitation, and Bert followed in his steps. They arrived in the sitting-room and looked about them.

"It's no good beating about the bush, Penn. You know what I'm after, but you and her family have put her under cover and it won't answer. Tulliver will have told you that. He's a good law-man and Copper rang him promptly."

"And what do you propose to do?" Robert asked.

"I'm not here to waste time, for a start. The little bitch was clever enough to see that her money was tied, or the Rudds were – or Tulliver. Your guess is as good as mine."

"By rights she should be in Scotland with you," Robert said, and Donald was sharp back with a reply to that.

"I'm not here to waste my time. She's not far away. I'll find her."

Bert was beginning to move round the room, his

181

squinting eye tilted everywhere to seek. I noticed that Robert moved back to the staircase, to block the way to the galley, but still I could see most of what happened.

"If we find her, we take her, but I'm willing to sell you grounds for a divorce from my legal wife, if that's what you want, and it's common knowledge you want her at any price. You're a wealthy man, Commander Penn."

"And then the blackmail would start. Don't take me for a fool. I want nothing from you and you're playing with fire."

"It's my guess the lifeboat clique have surrounded her with barb' wire," Bert growled, "but they can't keep her hid for ever. The Don has his rights by British Law, and we have mates who could find her and do a removal job on her permanent."

"It was easy, I thought at first," Donnie said. "We took off for London to finish the business end of all the things. I'd like to have seen her face when we didn't appear back on the ferry at Ruadh. You should have seen mine when I realised I had jumped too soon. I'm making you a fair offer, Commander – or else come and beg for her when I lay my hands on her."

"She's about here somewhere," Bert said, and moved towards the stairs. "Let's turn this place over, and then we can try the cottage."

"You're walking into trouble, Major. You really are a bastard. Did your wife ever see this side of your second-best character?"

Donnie's face was white, and he had picked up the car-keys and was rolling them in his hand. He threw them up and caught them again, and they flashed out a warning.

"This is a waste of time. Let's try the Cottage. I'd like leave to borrow your car."

"There's no chance of your taking my car."

"Come on, Bert. Let's go."

There was no time to see what happened. They were down the stairs, and the door was open and they were through.

"Don't go near the car, Conningsby," Robert shouted, "it's not safe."

He came running up the stairs and went past me to the square port that commanded the drive. In a moment he had it open, and I was out of the galley a few stairs below where he stood, his mouth cupped in his hands.

"Come back, Conningsby, don't try to use that car. It's not safe. Come back, for God's sake."

There was a wind that took the words and blew them with the dead leaves, stole all sound to inland away from the sea. There was no noise of the car starting, even in this direction of the near gale. The car moved on towards the cliff, quite slowly and so smoothly. Then it was at the head of the rise. It gained momentum, and it ran fast and faster, right to the edge, and all I could hear was Robert's shouted warnings that the brakes were gone. The grace that was a vintage Rolls coupé tilted at the very edge, and there was a fearful last beauty about her as she slid into the sea.

"There's no time left, Copper. It's all run out. Let's go."

He took my hand in his, and we raced for the cliff edge. I knew better than he that there had never been an escape from the Drowning Hole. Sailors called it 'the bottomless pit', and it was a fearsome place. The car would have plunged deep, and the tide was running full. There were waves washing up against the cliff as if they reached for the low clouds that raced across the moon. I thought that all the white horses had got encircled in that one place and were galloping about and about, tossing their manes, their eyes wild with fear.

"It's what Noah calls an impossible sea," Robert said. "It's time we called him, the police too, but get one thing into your head, it's done."

He put his arm about me and took me back to the house, and there were shadows in the garden, that might be people, who came and whispered and disappeared again, but my thoughts were as wild as the white horses. I stood by the telephone and listened to the telephone calls, and presently, maybe, I heard the maroons go. Yet I would have sworn that I saw my father down by the gate as we came in. It might have been a plane breaking the sound barrier and I was losing patches of time.

Robert found me with my head in my hands at the glass table, and I wondered if the red-red-red of the precious stone still shone in the deeps.

"Galatea," he said. "It's best if you turn into stone for a while. "You've just lost your husband in an accident, and I give you my word it was an accident. It was planned, but not like this. I don't think they knew the car was there, except Jimma Grimes, maybe a few people, who had nothing to do with it ..."

He stopped sharply and then spoke again.

"I admit there were men out there tonight. The Major wouldn't have got far, but I think that God remembered that vengeance was his. Gran would have liked that."

There would be an inquest, and Gran would never lie on oath. She appeared through the front door in the navy reefer coat with the brass buttons, and she kissed my cheek and offered me sympathy for my loss. She might have seen

184

me half an hour since, by her manner.

"Mary Canning is at Flint Cottage," she said. "She dropped in at ours, while Copper came on here. Did Major Conningsby come looking for his wife?"

I saw them constructing what had actually happened and putting a spin to it, that could be true.

"He were always a masterful man – daresay he took the car without asking permission."

"I don't think they heard. The wind was strong and it carried the voice away. There was no chance ... They were so quick."

"Always masterful," Gran said again.

Gran could have told them the car was not safe. She had been down to Grimes, the Butcher's, after tea to buy sausages. Billy had told her that the Rolls' brakes were gone. "Uncle Jimma had parked the car safe at the bottom of the dip and he was to fix them first thing tomorra'.

"Commander Penn knew you've got to back out from the dip and sweep out the front gate, but the Major was a foreigner."

Then Gran had me in her arms, and I could feel the fortress that she was.

"There's life for you, Little Fish."

Then I could hardly hear her voice against my cheek.

"You'll have to accept it. You're a widow, and nobody in Marram knows what your wedding turned out to be, but it's done now. Them that asks no questions isn't told a lie – only what Miss Canning chooses to call the Flint Cottage Mob. That girl knows how to keep her pert tongue quiet. The Scots islanders won't be involved. They know nothing, and what was there to know?"

She smiled at me and told me it was time I came home. She'd wait for me down by the white gate, but first she'd walk up the cliff to watch the lifeboat trying to lift the car.

"You can see the lights, and your father went out with the boat. By rights, Copper and I would be up by the gap, but this is one rescue she mustn't see."

"The Almighty may have owed the Rudd's a debt, but He ped it," she said, and said "Thank 'ee" to Robert and took herself off.

There was a time when nobody was there but Robert, and he was very gentle with me.

"There's your benefactor, not I," he said, and smiled. "She was your guardian. From the day you were born, she was your guardian. I just pushed my way in as a co-guardian. She said nothing. Her signature was necessary on every legal deed to do with you, but none of us appreciated it. It was only after a while they found out, and all the transfer of assets was frozen. You've never appreciated Gran."

"Have I not?" I asked him. "Have I not indeed?"

"She'd have killed Conningsby rather than have harm come to you. Any of them would. People don't realise the breeding of the ones who go down to what we call the great waters."

There was a pause when he whispered that he loved me and would wed me if only I'd have him. Then Gran was waiting for me, having visited the cliff, and ended up in a shadow committee meeting by the white gate. Soon there would be people, yet Robert seemed to be unhurried. His voice was so low that I had to train my ears to hear him.

"There was a time once when I caught a sea-gull. I was too young not to have more sense. I tied a chunk of meat on

186

the end of a string and left it on a cliff ledge. The sea-gull swooped down and gulped and was prisoner, but as soon as I had her in my hands I knew what remorse was. I cradled her against my breast and knew agony, but there was a way out of it – soon done. I had a Scout knife, and I cut the string at her beak, opened my hands and let her free to the sky."

There was a long pause, and I could see the reflections of light from the sea below the cliff, see dark figures on the cliff edge. Time was running out.

He cast his eyes on the North Pole Star.

"Somebody let me go free tonight," he said. "I know exactly how the gull felt, and all the people who might have had him on a string."

He looked down at me, as he quoted the words softly,

"Them that ask no questions, isn't told a lie,
Watch the wall, my darling, while the gentlemen go by.
Five and twenty ponies,
Trotting through the dark.
Brandy for the Parson,
Baccy for the clerk.
Laces for a lady,
Letters for a spy,
Watch the wall, my darling, while the gentlemen go by."

Gran was signalling for me to make haste, and the police car was coming up the drive. It was all about to start, and still Robert's whisper as his lips brushed my cheek. I will always wonder if I really did understand what he said, or what he meant.

"They went by tonight again, like ghosts from the past.

187

They were there, if we needed them. I don't think we needed them, but they were there. Didn't you hear the jingle of the harness of five and twenty ponies, my darling, who went trotting through the dark?''